Other Books by Gene Masters

Silent Warriors: Submarine Warfare in the Pacific

Operation Exodus

The Laconia Incident

The Wounds of Jonas Clark

The Dry Cleaner: A Rich Vitelli Mystery

True Believers

Bobby Doyle is Missing

A Rich Vitelli Mystery

by

Gene Masters

Published by Escarpment Press

www.escarpmentpress.weebly.com
INDIAN LAND, SC

Chapter 1

It was the best run the professional football Marauders had made since the city was awarded a league franchise six years ago. Here it was, not halfway into the regular season, and the team was 6-1, and at the top of its division. Also, by all accounts, it was all due to the brilliant play of its rookie quarterback, Bobby Doyle, out of Boston College.

Frank Daugherty, the spokesman for the consortium that owned the team, had credited the team's coach and general manager, Jesse James Ferguson, with his wise selection of the underrated young black quarterback in the eleventh round of the previous draft.

"I saw that the kid had what it takes to be great," Ferguson was quoted as saying. "All he needed was a good enough offensive line in front of him, and a couple of decent receivers. BC didn't have them, but, thanks to a couple of other good picks, the Marauders do!"

The truth was that the team desperately needed a halfway decent backup for its franchise quarterback, Donny Nolan, and Doyle was the only halfway decent quarterback left in the eleventh round. But what if Nolan had not broken his collarbone on the team's first seasonal outing, and if Doyle had not won the game going away in relief? Wouldn't Doyle still be warming the bench behind whomever the team got to replace Nolan? But, sometimes, bad luck just brings on better luck, and Nolan's ill fortune was the Marauders' gain.

Doyle played brilliantly in the next two games as well, and the Marauders won both of them going away.

But the Marauders' good fortune would soon take a turn for the worse.

Chapter 2

It was a pretty elaborate plan, even if Alvaro said so himself. Alvaro Gomez had it in for Bobby Doyle ever since Doyle had ruined Alvaro's baby sister, Elaina's, life. That was back in Doyle's junior year at Boston College. Of course, Elaina was equally to blame, even if Alvaro refused to admit it—a freshman English Lit major going bananas over her team's quarterback was just stupid. She told Alvaro that she had met Doyle at a party one night, and they both had had too much to drink. "It just happened," she said, "and only that one time. When I told him afterward, when I found out I was pregnant, he said it couldn't be his, and maybe I should think about getting rid of it. But I could never have done that."

So it was that Gomez's baby sister admittedly did a stupid thing, and she was resigned to living with the consequences of her actions. But, as Alvaro saw things, there was still no excuse for the way Doyle took advantage of Elaina. He had used her, and then discarded her like a dirty Kleenex. But Alvaro was going to get even for that. He was going to make Bobby Doyle pay for what he had done to his sister.

Oh, he knew the line—the nuns who taught him in grade school had drummed it into him—"Revenge is mine, sayeth the Lord."

Well, now Alvaro intended to give the Lord a little help.

Chapter 3

When all this began, Alvaro had just begun his job as an apprentice welder at Bath Iron Works in Maine. Bath was just 130 miles north of Roxbury, in Boston, where Alvaro, Elaina, and their older sister Juana, were born and raised. About the same time, Bobby Doyle, also from Roxbury, both black and a Catholic, was awarded a scholarship to Boston Memorial Catholic. At BMC, Bobby excelled not only on the school's football team, but also on the running track and on the basketball court.

Elaina was still in the seventh grade at the time, in Dearborn Middle School in Roxbury. She was bright, and Dearborn was one of the best public schools in the area; Alvaro, not so much, but he had already decided by then that all he wanted was to work with his hands. He enrolled in Boston Joint Apprentice Training Center (JACT) in nearby Dorchester, where he took up welding.

Then each of the three went on to do their own thing: both Bobby and Elaina went on to Boston College, and Alvaro went up to Bath.

PUERTO RICANS COME FROM some tightly knit families, and the Gomez family was no exception. Alvaro was not much of a letter writer — who is these days? — but he called home regularly, not just because *Mami*, Violetta Gomez, expected it, but also because it would never occur to Alvaro to ever let *Mami* down. So, when Elaina dropped out of BC because she was pregnant, Alvaro heard about it right away. And he was on the next bus back to Boston.

Violetta and *Papi* (Jorge Gomez) were beside themselves. Elaina was spending most of her time crying in the room she used to share with her big sister, Juana. Of course, she had lost her scholarship when she dropped out of school, and she could not seem to hold a job. Eventually, Elaina just moped about the house, depressed, and she ate. And she got very big — not just pregnant big.

Juana, who had also disappointed her parents by running off and marrying (in Alvaro's considered opinion, a good-for-nothing *cerdo*) Peter Vargas, would now make sarcastic remarks. She would go on about how *Papi*'s pride and joy, his blessed Elaina, had *really* disgraced the family. Alvaro countered with "So Juana, we should be so proud because you, at least, ran off and *married* Vargas after you slept with him?"

The more Elaina moped, the more Alvaro became ever more obsessed with "getting even," and punishing Bobby Doyle. He brooded, thinking of ways to make Doyle suffer for what he had done to his baby sister.

After that, most weeks, Alvaro would come back home to be with the family. He was making good money by then, and could afford to buy a decent used car, so at least he did not have to depend on the bus schedules. When he thought he had accumulated enough cash to pay a lawyer, he visited one, asking what he could legally do to make Bobby Doyle pay for ruining Elaina's life.

"Wait 'til the child is born," Anthony J. Reilly, Esq., explained. "DNA testing will prove beyond doubt that Doyle is the father. You *are* sure that Doyle is the father, aren't you?" the lawyer asked.

"No doubt whatsoever," Alvaro replied, and the suit was filed.

The following month, Bobby Doyle was stopped on the Boston College Newton campus while walking between classes. A young woman he did not know stopped him, and thrust a large envelope into his hand. When he took it with a confused look, she said "You have been served," and then turned and walked away. Opening the envelope, Doyle was nonplussed, discovering that he was being sued.

Once the suit was filed, Alvaro decided to hold Doyle's feet to the fire, and released copies of the filing of the filing to both the *Boston Globe* and the *Boston Herald*. Both newspapers called the Gomez residence, asking to interview Elaina. Jorge intercepted their calls and impolitely refused. Doyle, apparently, had been less reticent, and issued a statement that he was completely innocent of the charges.

Both papers went on to publish the fact that Doyle had been sued over the paternity of the unborn child of Elaina Gomez, and when questioned, Doyle denied that the suit had any substance. Ms. Gomez, however, had refused to issue a statement.

A representative of the Boston College administration, also asked for comment, said they never commented on ongoing litigation. But they also would not comment on any decision as to whether Doyle would remain on the football team, and play out his senior year.

What thus might have been a major news story, because of Elaina's reticence, was relegated to two short paragraphs on the second and third pages of the respective newspapers. Bobby Doyle's college football career, meanwhile, never actually skipped a beat; for the time being, at least, he kept his scholarship and practiced with the team. And Alvaro was even more incensed at his failure to make Bobby Doyle suffer in the least for what he had done.

Chapter 4

Things at the Gomez home got steadily worse thereafter. Elaina had carried her child for five months, at which point she said she could no longer feel the baby move inside her. Her doctor, not hearing a heartbeat, did some further tests, and told Elaina that sadly her baby had died inside her. She then learned that she would have to carry the child to term, and deliver a stillborn. With that, Elaina went into what the doctor said was "severe depression," and grew even fatter. Jorge, in turn, not only worried about Elaina's mental state, he mourned the loss of a prospective grandchild. Jorge already had had one heart attack, and his preexisting heart problem got worse and worse.

Violetta called in their parish priest, Father Gilligan, to come to the house and counsel Elaina. He did, and after a session with her, told both parents that Elaina was obviously clinically depressed, and the she needed more professional help than he could provide. He suggested they contact Catholic Charities Boston, which would provide professional counseling for free. But Jorge balked, saying, "Bringing in the priest is one thing, taking charity another. I will not hang our dirty laundry out in public!"

Meanwhile, Alvaro was doing really well on the job, and had risen quickly from apprentice to journeyman. He would lose himself and his troubles daily, concentrating on nothing else but the laying down of smooth, continuous beads of weld, taking great satisfaction in the quality of his work. The good money he had been making grew even better. Never a gregarious individual, he had no life outside of work, and he just kept salting his wages away. Pretty soon, he had built up what anyone would consider a small fortune in his bank account.

Then he got a call from Violetta that they had found Elaina in the bathtub with her wrists slit. Luckily, they had found her before she bled out, and the EMTs had gotten her to the hospital in time to save her. "Oh yeah," Violetta said, "and the whole thing gave *Papi* another heart attack—but he is home, now, and he's okay."

Jorge could not have been all that okay, because right after Elaina was transferred into rehab, he had another—this time massive—heart attack, and died. It was just one more thing Alvaro considered Bobby Doyle had to answer for.

Somehow, in rehab, Elaina got hold of some pills. This time, they did *not* find her in time. They buried her just two weeks after they buried Jorge. Now, for all that, Alvaro determined that Bobby Doyle had to die!

With Elaina gone, it became senseless to retain Anthony J. Reilly, Esq. No longer on retainer, and with the cause for any legal redress now moot, Reilly formally withdrew the suit. With that, the Boston College administration quietly told Doyle that he could remain on the team, and play his senior year.

Soon afterward, Alvaro passed the Master Welder certification test. Then, Violetta, now living all by herself, decided to give up their apartment and move in with Juana and Pete. Alvaro, who could never stand being around his brother-in-law, could not fathom how his *Mami* was able to stomach Pete, much less live with him. Alvaro decided, therefore, that he did not even have a home to come and visit on weekends.

Through all of this, the image of Bobby Doyle was never far from Alvaro's mind. Bobby Doyle, and Bobby Doyle alone, was responsible for the misery his mindless seduction of Alvaro's baby sister had brought down on Alvaro's family. And now that he was a master welder, with a very healthy bank account, Alvaro enacted a scheme that would make Bobby Doyle pay with his life.

But now he also decided, that before he killed him, Bobby Doyle would know why his life was forfeit, and maybe even *beg* Alvaro to kill him. *Dying is too easy*, Alvaro thought, *Bobby Doyle must be made to* suffer *first*.

Chapter 5

"Bobby Doyle is missing," Johnny Fowler said when Rich Vitelli showed up at Metro Police headquarters that Wednesday morning.

"What?" Vitelli questioned. "You're kidding, right? Our Marauders star quarterback?"

"The very same," Fowler answered. "The Captain said he would fill you in on the details, and he wants to see you right away!"

"Guess that means I get my coffee later," Vitelli said with a smirk, as he made his way to his boss's office. He rapped on Captain Parker's rickety, glass-paneled office door, and found Parker sitting behind his ancient mahogany desk, head down, looking even smaller than his "maybe" five foot five frame.

"What's up, chief?" Vitelli asked.

Parker had been head of Metro Police Missing Persons for three years before Vitelli had transferred over from Homicide. That was just over six years ago. Vitelli's wife, Margie, had been diagnosed with terminal cancer, and Vitelli's response to his wife's suffering was to throw himself into his work. He had been hard at it, working on a particularly nasty homicide case, when he was notified that she was in her hospital room, dying, and asking for him. Unfortunately, he arrived too late to be there when she passed. It was remorse that caused him to abandon the frenetic pace of Homicide and transfer to the relatively slower world of Missing Persons. And nobody was happier to get him then Parker, although you would never know it from the way he greeted Vitelli that particular morning:

"Nice of you to join us this morning, Lieutenant!" Parker said, without even looking up. Parker's peripatetic disposition was a thing of legend throughout Metro. But it was a side of him that Vitelli rarely saw, because, in fact, Parker genuinely liked and respected Vitelli—and rightly so, given Vitelli's job performance.

Before leaving Tuesday evening, Vitelli had told his boss that he needed to drop his car off for service that morning, and Parker had just nodded. Vitelli's Nissan Rogue had been stalling at traffic lights for months, and it was *past* time for service. Vitelli also knew that reminding Parker that he given him tacit permission for his tardiness would be a waste of time.

"Good morning, Captain! I understand that our star quarterback has gone missing."

Parker looked up from his desk at his ace detective, noting that he looked a lot more fit these days, for whatever reason. Otherwise, the same old Vitelli: black hair, grey at the temples and starting to thin; dressed in his usual business casual, blue shirt, solid maroon tie, khaki slacks. Parker rarely rose from his desk when Vitelli came onto his office. At six-two, Vitelli towered over his diminutive boss.

"Coach Ferguson filed the paperwork this morning. Seems he was supposed to report to practice yesterday morning, and never showed. Ferguson says that wasn't like Doyle at all, so he sent somebody to Doyle's place over at the Hamilton Arms to see if he was all right. They found his bed hadn't been slept in, and the CCTV recordings don't show him ever coming back after he left to go out last Sunday evening. Apparently, it was his habit to go out and tip a few after a game."

"And the coaching staff allowed that?"

"When you're the star quarterback and win games, you apparently get to do pretty much whatever you please, I guess."

"I guess. Did anybody stop to think that maybe Doyle got lucky Sunday night, and just lost track of time?"

"I asked that very same question," Parker replied, with a smirk, "and Ferguson told me that while Doyle 'got lucky' quite regularly, it never, ever, caused him to miss practice before. Not ever. No matter what, Doyle apparently *never* missed practice. No, Ferguson was pretty adamant that something bad had happened to Doyle." Parker paused, perhaps to let that bit of information sink in.

"Get on it, Detective, find Doyle, and quick, before the feds muscle in on the case. Here's the file. Not much in it," he said, as he handed the thin file folder to Vitelli.

Vitelli mulled the situation over as he filled his coffee mug and sidled over to his own desk, next to the nearly opaque window in the corner of the office. Doyle had been spectacular in the previous Sunday's game, and in the other seven games the Marauders had played since the season opener. *And they would have won the one game they lost, if Martinelli hadn't dropped Doyle's bullet in the end zone at the end of the fourth. And then, with just fourteen seconds left to play, if our never-miss kicker hadn't blown a chip-shot field goal from the thirty-yard line. My guess is that if we don't find Doyle fast, and alive and well, there won't be much of a season left for the home team.*

Chapter 6

Alvaro remembered how the Boston papers got all worked up about how the Marauders had drafted Bobby Doyle, albeit not until the eleventh round. *Local boy makes good, and all that crap.* But for Alvaro, all it meant was that he had to put in his notice at Bath, and find a new job on the Marauders' home turf.

He got lucky. Working through his local union at Bath, he found a job interview in the city within a week. The boss at Elegance Yachts, one Ezra Farnsworth, bald and plump, shorter even than Alvaro, was blown away when he demonstrated the welding skills he had perfected at Bath. Farnsworth hired him on the spot. Alvaro took a pay cut compared to Bath, but Elegance was willing to pay him well over the going union rate for master welders in the area. In any case, the cost of living was much lower there than in the tax-happy New England area.

Now, all he had to do was set his plan in motion.

He had already accomplished quite a bit when Doyle reported to the Marauders' camp for spring training. Since he was not supposed to be their starting quarterback, he hadn't received any media attention. That was just fine by Alvaro. It would be easier to waylay him, and there would not be the same public panic if just a *backup* quarterback went missing. But that changed big time after the season started, and Doyle took over from Nolan. So, it did not work out exactly the way he had envisioned, but, for Alvaro, all it meant was just another complication among many. Bobby Doyle would be a dead man, no matter what.

Finding an empty warehouse was easy enough—even one out of the way. Alvaro took a six-month lease on a smallish place northeast of downtown, in the boonies. Even so, the first month's rent, and the security deposit, had taken a big chunk out of his savings. Setting it up for his own needs was simple: the warehouse office had space for a cot, and it already had a small lunch room with a sink and a refrigerator. All he added was a microwave. There was even a toilet with a stall shower. He bailed out of the cheap motel he had been living in, and moved into the warehouse.

Setting the place up for the time Doyle would spend there, was another matter altogether.

First of all, even as remote as the location was, he could not take the chance that a screaming prisoner would attract the attention of any passersby. The place, small as warehouses go, was still a huge sound chamber. A shouted word would bounce around inside the building and be magnified. There was nothing else for it: Doyle's jail cell would have to be enclosed in a soundproof room. Now although Alvaro knew from welding, he knew nothing whatever about sound propagation and dampening. So he spent a couple weeks after work, in the library, reading up on the subject. In the end, he could tell you all about decibels, sound waves, and sympathetic vibrations. And he could sketch a soundproof room, built with materials he could order from Lowe's.

He worked after hours and on weekends, and in all kinds of weather, and by the time the Marauders were well into their season, Alvaro had Doyle's prison ready.

Inside the soundproof room Alvaro had built on the warehouse floor was a cage, fashioned from welded number-five rebar. The bars were spaced four inches apart vertically, and were welded to horizontal crosspieces located every foot, starting at the floor. The cage, with its rebar sides and roof, was chain-welded to a floor made from butt-welded, half-inch steel plates. As usual, the weld lines Alvaro laid down were things of beauty to behold!

There was a double-padlocked door, which swung on fabricated hinges. There was a horizontal opening, three-feet wide and just off the floor, and barely wide enough to pass food trays through. A steel shuttle chamber in the far corner held the slop bucket. It may have been ugly as sin, but, to Alvaro, the cage was a thing of beauty: a master welder's dream.

Now, all it needed was an occupant.

Chapter 7

All Bobby Doyle could remember about the night before was the little Hispanic guy who had befriended him and was buying the drinks. *The little prick must have put something in one of them,* he thought. *I remember him telling me he needed to drive me home and asking me for my keys. And like an idiot I gave them to him, and even walked out with him and showed him where the car was.*

It was only then that Doyle realized that he was stretched out on a slab of something cold, hard, and metallic. He opened his eyes. Wherever he was, it was not home, and it was pretty dimly lighted. He was, indeed, he noted, lying on a metal floor. His head hurt, and he was woozy—not drunk woozy, not alcohol woozy, but drug woozy. *"The little prick" had indeed slipped something into that last drink!* He raised his head, and it hurt even worse, but at least he could see his surroundings, maybe even figure out where he was. And where he was proved to be weird as hell.

He was in a cage! And there were padlocks on the door! He had been caged up like some zoo animal, a prize cat, or something! *What the hell is going on? And where in the hell am I?*

And then Bobby Doyle, confused and overwhelmed, lowered his head and fell back into a logy sleep.

Chapter 8

The media jumped on the Doyle story as soon as the Marauders released the statement that Tuesday morning that their star quarterback had gone missing. The city's lone newspaper could report about nothing else for days afterward, and the local and national electronic news was also all over the story.

The Marauders published a nationwide appeal to the public for anyone having any information as to Bobby Doyle's whereabouts. A fifty-thousand-dollar reward was immediately offered by the club for any information that led to Doyle's safe recovery. The Marauder management set up a reporting hotline, monitored 24/7.

For Vitelli, all this activity promised to hinder his investigation every bit as much as it might help it. *And just a fifty grand reward for your star quarterback? Why so chintzy?* But his boss, Captain Parker, was particularly happy that the football club, and not the Metro Police Department, had set up, was manning, and, especially, *paying for,* the hotline.

The crap that was being recorded off the hotline, however, was originally being sifted through first by the hotline operators. Then, only "what they thought might be important" was turned over to police Missing Persons (*i.e.,* Vitelli and Johnny Fowler). It took some time for Vitelli to get through to Marauder management that the police needed to hear *everything* that was reported. After that, they got unedited copies of the recordings; it was still all pretty much crap.

But then around noon on Wednesday, a person named Arnold Schuster reported that he was in a sports bar in East Lakeside the previous Sunday evening, a place called "Half Time," when Bobby Doyle had showed up around ten.

Schuster went on to report that "Everybody in the place crowded around Bobby, congratulating him on the team's victory, and offered to buy him drinks. But Doyle took a shine to this one Hispanic guy—seems the kid was from Bobby's old neighborhood in Boston—and they started drinking together. Not too long after that, Bobby was high as a kite, and the kid was walking him out of the place. Bobby, ya know, waving to everyone, telling them to have a good time. And that his 'new good buddy' was gonna drive him home. And that's the last we saw of him."

Vitelli spent the rest of the afternoon finding Schuster, and arranged to talk to him that very day.

"SO, DETECTIVE, YOU THINK I got a shot at collecting that fifty large?" Arnold Schuster asked Vitelli, right after he gave him permission to record their conversation. Schuster had checked out the cop, wondering if he could be straight with him. He figured Vitelli to be early to mid-forties, about 200 pounds, taller than he was, dressed nice at least. His black hair was starting to thin, grey at the temples, brown eyes. *Bet this guy gets all the tail he wants,* Schuster mused. *That hang-dog look gets 'em every time!*

Vitelli eyed Schuster in turn: thin, six feet, maybe 180 pounds, pinched face, hawkish nose, long and unruly brown hair—a *guy who plays all the angles*—his first impression, almost always accurate.

"Like I told the guy on the phone," Schuster was saying, "Bobby Doyle comes into the Half Time 'bout ten o'clock. Of course, everybody in the place recognizes him, and wants to buy him a round—me included, you know—when this little guy, swarthy complexion, pimp moustache, says to Doyle, 'Hey, man, ain't you from Roxbury?' and Bobby says, 'Yeah,' and they go on from there like it was old home week, and they'd known each other for ages. Doesn't take Bobby long to get blitzed, though—hell, it wasn't even close to midnight yet—and the little guy is walking Bobby out to his car to drive him home. Least, that's what everyone thought he was doing. Only found out this morning that Bobby had gone missing. Had to be that little prick what done it.

"Say, Lieutenant," Schuster continued, "how come only a fifty grand reward, anyway? You'd think the Marauders would offer a hell of a lot more to get their main man back, wouldn't you?"

"You'd have to ask the team management about that, Mr. Schuster," Vitelli said. "Okay, can you tell me a bit more about the little guy who left the bar with Doyle? How small was he? Height? Weight?"

"Okay. Kid was built like a middleweight—not my height, half-a-head shorter maybe, and skinny—I'd say one thirty to one forty. Like I said, he had this thin moustache."

"Hair color? Eye color?"

"Hair black and slick, kinda. Wore it long, had a pigtail. His eyes were dark—maybe brown."

"Okay, that's good. Did you see or hear anything else that might help? Tattoos maybe?"

"No, Detective, not really. Oh, yeah, he had a gold earring in his left ear—little gold ring."

"Excellent! Do you think you could remember what he looked like enough to work with our police sketch artist?

"Yeah, sure. I'd be happy to do that!"

"Very well, Mr. Schuster, I'll turn you over to Detective Fowler then, and he'll set you up with the police artist. And thank you for coming in."

"No problem. Do I got a shot at that reward? Maybe fifty large ain't much for getting their guy back, but, still, collecting it would be better than getting a sharp stick in the eye!"

"That is not up to me, Mr. Schuster. Since you called in, two other people who were also at the bar called in, and they have yet to be interviewed. What needs to happen is that we need to find Mr. Doyle based on your deposition."

Later, at least two other callers who also were in the Half Time bar Sunday night, pretty much confirmed Schuster's story. Neither one, however, was able to provide anywhere as much detail as to "the little Hispanic guy's" appearance as Schuster had. They did confirm, however, that the police artist's sketch based on Schuster's description did resemble the man they had seen.

The sketch showed a thin-faced man, with a long, thin, prominent nose, high cheek bones, dark eyes. His mouth was small for the face; thick lips, with a thin moustache clinging to the upper lip; dark hair pulled back from the face as if tied in the back, making the ears prominent; an earring, a ring, in the left earlobe.

That evening, the sketch of a "person of interest" in the Doyle disappearance was released to the media.

Chapter 9

Anubis Cline stood to lose a great deal of money, one way or the other, unless Bobby Doyle was found, and found quickly. Anubis Cline did *not* like to lose money.

Cline was just coming out of a year's purple funk: the depression into which he had retreated after the murder of his blind ward, Jael.

That event had taken place the better part of a year earlier, when a woman named Charlene Morton broke into Cline's West Lakeside home. Morton, a close associate of the murdered Sheldon Hertz, one of Cline's clients, was certain that it was Cline who had arranged Hertz's death, and she was bent on killing him in turn.

Knife in hand, she had attacked Cline in his bed. As fate would have it, however, she was well into accomplishing her goal when Cline's beloved ward, Jael, attacked Morton, pulling her off Cline. Morton, striking back at Jael, then stabbed Jael fatally.

Cline, in turn, now given the time to retrieve a pistol from his bedstand, shot Morton, killing her.

The police investigation concluded that Cline had acted in self defense. His vindication, however, had never sat well with Vitelli, who was certain that it was Cline who had arranged for the murder of Sheldon Hertz to begin with—the very murder for which Morton had vengefully attacked Cline. While Vitelli shared Morton's certainty that Cline was responsible for Hertz's death, the one witness who might have fingered Cline for the murder had mysteriously turned up dead from a drug overdose—even though he had no history of drug use. There had been all too many convenient coincidences, and Vitelli believed there was no such thing as a coincidence—never mind a whole string of them. Cline was at the root of all this skullduggery. Vitelli was sure of it, he just couldn't prove it

But that was then. It had taken an entire year for Cline to come to terms with the loss of his beloved ward, but come to terms with it he did — in his own peculiar way. His recourse, finally, was simply to resurrect her in his mind whenever the occasion called for it.

When Jael was alive, he would frequently discuss situations and opportunities with her. Jael would be his sounding board for his various schemes and plots. Her value lay in what, to his mind, was her complete objectivity. Like him, she had the complete inability to shrink away from pursuing the most expeditious course of action, no matter how illegal or immoral.

Anubis Cline, now done with mourning, was back into something more like his old self, and was ready to move on. And if Bobby Doyle was not found — and found quickly, before next Sunday's game, if at all possible — Cline stood to lose a great deal of money. And even back when he was in the throes of depression, Anubis Cline *hated* losing money.

Anubis Cline sat in his office chair, an unlit black cigar clenched in his yellowed teeth, holding an entirely imagined conversation with his deceased ward:

The Metro Police Department is a reasonably effective force, but is legally restricted in what it can do. The police must, after all, obey the law, follow procedure, observe the rules. One can operate so much more quickly and effectively if one bends the law just a little here and there. And I know just the man.

"*Who do you mean, Abba?*" Jael responded in his mind's eye. "*Surely not the Russian. He will betray you at his first opportunity!*"

Of course, he will, my Dear. But don't you see? That is the beauty of it! It is only important that he find Doyle expeditiously — as quickly as possible — and the Russian has the ways and means to

do just that. If Doyle is found and returned unhurt, then the Marauders will most likely have an excellent season. If he's found dead, then we can at least deal with that. But if not found, either dead or alive, then the situation remains in Limbo. The team will probably lose games, and continue to lose them, and finish the season out of the money. And whenever and however the team loses money, we lose money!

"*But the Russian! If he finds Doyle dead, then no matter. Dead is dead, and cannot be changed. But if he finds Doyle alive, then he can extort money or other concessions from you for returning him to you alive.*"

And I will, of course, refuse.

"*Then he will either kill him, or worse, release him so maimed that he can never play again!*"

Of course he will, my Dear, of course he will. And I have been long prepared for either such eventuality!

"*Ah, Abba, you are so clever!*"

Cline then placed a phone call to Viktor Korborov on his secure line.

Chapter 10

Bobby Doyle came awake again, totally unaware that he had been out for an entire day and night since he had first awakened and found himself locked in a steel cage. His body had almost completely metabolized the drug by then, and, this time, he awoke alert. Unfortunately, opening his eyes and seeing his surroundings, he noted, *Shit! It wasn't a dream! I really* am *in some kind of steel cage.* And he had to pee. Badly.

He looked around some more. In the cage with him were a plastic, gallon-sized bottle of water and a plate of food: a McMuffin of some vintage, in its original McDonald's wrapping.

"Thought you might be hungry," a voice came from the corner of the room, a South Boston accent somewhat like his own. "And thirsty," it added.

"Got to piss," Doyle answered.

"Bucket. In the corner," came the reply.

Reluctantly, Doyle got up and stretched out his heavily muscled six-foot, six-inch frame, finding his head could almost touch the overhead bars. He was a handsome man, tight black curls close-cropped, dark eyes the same color as his captor. He wore the same casual clothes he was wearing when he was abducted: tan slacks, bleached denim shirt, tasseled loafers—now much the worse for wear. He went to the corner and used the bucket, sighing with relief as he did. Then he went over to the water bottle and drank greedily. Next, he picked up and examined the McMuffin, and opened the package. He took a test bite. Egg, sausage, and cheese. "Cold," he said.

"What do you expect?" the man said. "You've been asleep since I got here."

"Yeah, well. Look, I'm gonna need more to eat than this. And I need protein—at least a hundred grams a day—or I'll begin losing muscle."

"You'll eat whatever I bring you. Besides, you won't have to worry about that much longer."

"What? What is *that* supposed to mean? And who *are* you, and why am I locked up like this?"

Alvaro stepped into the light, and Doyle saw a short, thin man with a dark complexion, aquiline features, long black hair, and a thin moustache over his upper lip. He wore a tiny gold ring in his left ear. He was in work clothes: blue denim shirt and jeans, steel-toed, dark brown work boots. "I am Alvaro Gomez," he said, "and you are here so I can kill you. And I will kill you because you murdered to my sister."

"What?" Doyle said. "I haven't the slightest idea who you are, or who your sister is. And I never murdered anybody."

"Oh, but you did, Bobby Doyle," Alvaro replied, angrily. "You murdered her just as surely as if you shot her with a gun. And, before that, you killed my father."

"I never . . ." Doyle countered. "I don't know what you're talking about."

With that, Alvaro proceeded to tell him the long, sad, story of Elaina Gomez, her descent into Hell on Earth, and about his father's untimely fatal heart attack.

Chapter 11

The FBI had moved in on the Italian mob in the city a year or two back; they put their bosses into federal penitentiaries, and shut down many of their illegal operations in the city. It was then that the Russian mob, under Viktor Korborov, quickly moved in to fill the void.

Even before the FBI had thrown a wrench into their operation, the Italian mob had lately taken great pains to avoid public scrutiny; the murder and mayhem continued, of course, but it was just that every attempt was made to keep such goings-on out of the public eye. One of those efforts, for example, involved employing the services of the Dry Cleaner to completely dispose of inconvenient corpses.

The Russians, on the other hand, never had any such scruples. They took exactly the opposite tack. They thrived on operating out in the open—and viciously—striking terror into the public psyche. The more blood-covered corpses that were strewn on the city streets, the better. The Russian mob wanted, above all else, to be feared.

Of course, the FBI had zoned in on the Russian mob, but getting enough evidence to put Viktor Korborov away had, thus far, proved truly elusive. It had, to date, been impossible to find anyone who could directly testify against Korborov. Anyone with direct knowledge of his involvement in any particular crime, was either fiercely loyal to Korborov, or very afraid of him. Those individuals with such knowledge, who were either disloyal or unafraid, tended to be found very dead. Besides, these days, Korborov never did any of the required "wet work" himself; he had plenty of other people to do it for him.

Chapter 12

"Viktor?"

"Yes."

"It's Anubis Cline."

"Yes, *Mister* Cline. To what do I owe the honor?"

Korborov had met Cline in person only once, with a proposition for using some of Cline's business interests for money laundering. He could picture him in his mind's eye: a huge, round man, the impression of his bulk muting the man's actual short stature. Facial features like a bag of rocks: pig eyes set close together. Yet another picture came to mind, recalled from his youth in Volgograd, from one of the dubbed-in-Russian *Star Wars* movies he loved: the character Jabba the Hut. Cline was Jabba the Hut swathed in white linen.

"Have you thought again about my proposition?" said Viktor.

"I have, Viktor, and, as before, I don't believe the time is yet ripe for us to do that kind of business. And while it's perfectly clear that it would be mutually beneficial financially, I simply don't see how we could keep such cooperation out of the public eye. Face it, Victor, subtlety is not your organizational strong suit."

The comment, however merited, made Korborov seethe. "What do you want, then? he asked, testily.

"Your assistance in another matter altogether. You are aware of my business interest in the Marauders football team?"

"I am. I understand that you have controlling interest in the team. Although I could never understand why you Americans call the game 'football,'" he opined, "when it is played with the hands. But that is another matter."

On the other end of the line, Cline grunted, his version of a laugh. "Be that as it may, Viktor, the Marauders generate a very nice income stream, and the sudden disappearance of my star player threatens that income stream. I want you to help me by finding Bobby Doyle."

"Yes, I heard on the news that your star player is missing. Are not the police looking for him?"

"They are. But they are constrained by what they can legally do. You, on the other hand . . ."

"I understand. I observe no such limits. And if I find this Bobby Doyle?"

"I would be most grateful. Certainly grateful enough to rethink your business proposal."

"I see. A test." *That arrogant* svin'ya, he thought.

"Not at all. Call it an opportunity."

Opportunity my left nut, you pompous mu-dak! "Certainly, Mister Cline, I will do what I can."

"Excellent, Viktor. And time is of the essence. The sooner Bobby Doyle is back on the playing field, the better!"

"Yes. I will get my boys right on it."

"Thank you, Viktor. I appreciate that,"

No sooner had they hung up, than Viktor Korborov was considering ways to turn the "opportunity" to his advantage, and get a leg up on Anubis Cline.

Chapter 13

Vitelli headed home that evening, satisfied that his car was performing properly again. The dealer had found the problem that made his Rogue stall at traffic lights: a dirty fuel filter. What grated was that it should have been a simple and straightforward fix. Instead, the dealer explained, half the engine had to be disassembled to get to the filter. *So much for Japanese engineering!* Vitelli thought.

Vitelli lived in the Wildwood section of the city. It had been considered run-down when he bought into the neighborhood, and the apartment was cheap. But the area had since become gentrified, and now he could not have afforded to move there if he wasn't already living there. It was not much — a two-bedroom, two-bath, on the upper floor, western side, of a quadruplex — but it was clean and easy to keep that way. Perfect for him.

Except for two mature cats (Tristan and Isolde were litter mates his late wife brought home as kittens), he had lived alone since Margie had died. That was most likely because he had never met anyone after her who could begin to match her, and so he just stayed single. Lately, though, he was getting bouts of loneliness. *Perhaps,* he thought, *my little two-night stand with Leona Barrett — just one of her names I know, but the one I first knew the Dry Cleaner by — has awakened some unrealized deep-seated need for companionship?*

He had tried to fill the void with a badly needed exercise regimen: morning runs and three-a-week gym visits. He even started back to Sunday Mass most weekends. It all helped, but it did not quite do the job. *Maybe I should join a middle-aged singles club, or something!*

Although he was actually a pretty decent cook, Vitelli rarely cooked for himself; he lived mostly on takeout and frozen prepared meals. This night, it was one of the latter: Salisbury steak, with broccoli and mashed potatoes. He washed it down with a cold Semple's, a local pale lager brew he favored. Then he watched a fairly decent movie on Amazon Prime, the two cats cuddling next to him on the couch.

Getting ready for bed, he glanced at himself in the mirror. *I'm getting there. Still have some work to do, but my gut is slowly getting smaller!* He brushed his teeth and turned in.

Chapter 14

On Thursday, not one, but *three*, ransom notes were received: two were called into the Marauders' hotline, and one was mailed to the downtown Marauders' headquarters building at One Marauder Place. One of the calls was traced to a well-known nut case, who had been continually calling in to the Metro Police confessing to various crimes, real or imagined. He was picked up for questioning, but Vitelli knew nothing would come of it, and he was eventually released.

The second call was traced to a burner phone. The speaker demanded a million dollars for Doyle's return, and said he would call again at seven that evening with further instructions. Vitelli considered that the call might actually be authentic.

Finally, the mailed ransom demand (this one for two and a half million) was a paste-up job, demanding the Marauders organization set up a special phone number to be published in the local newspaper's classified ads. For Vitelli, this last demand, while possibly authentic, smacked of too much drama—like something out of a true-crime TV show—to be real.

Chief Parker was seriously upset when he heard about the ransom demands. "Crap!" he said to Vitelli. "Just what we need. Now Doyle's disappearance looks like a kidnapping, whether it really is or not! Crap!" Then, after a loud sigh, he said, "All right, Vitelli. Nothing for it, now. Got to bring in the damn feds. Call your black FBI buddy, whatshisname."

"It's Maddox. Will do, boss," said Vitelli, picturing Eric Maddox in his mind's eye: clear-eyed, exuding intelligence, movie star, leading man handsome. He then placed a call to

Maddox at the FBI building downtown. Maddox answered on the first ring.

"Eric?"

"Hey, Rich," Eric Maddox said into the telephone. "Already heard the news. One Marauder Place is as leaky as a sieve. Already have my people down there kicking the Marauders staffing off the hotline and setting up our own monitoring team. Surprised you didn't do that right off."

"Would have liked to," Vitelli replied testily, "but Missing Persons doesn't have the staff nor the budget. What we did get, at least, were the unedited phone recordings turned over to us at the end of every shift. And they did alert us right away to anything else they thought was really important. You know, like a ransom note?"

"Right."

"And I think you'll find that the Marauders' staff is very cooperative, even if it *is* leaky. They sent us over the original of that ransom note, for example. They were even careful to stop handling it after they saw what it was, and stick it into a clean file folder before they couriered it over. They want to find Bobby Doyle every bit as much as anybody in this city, and probably more"

"Okay, Rich. You sound upset. What have I said that upset you?"

"Nothing really, Eric. It's just this case. Doyle's been off the radar since last Sunday night, right after he turned in one of the best performances on the field in his career. Then, when he shows up missing on Tuesday, the Marauders organization sets up this hotline, but offers only fifty thousand dollars reward for his return? For their *star quarterback*? And, if this is a kidnapping—and I'm not saying it isn't—then why would a kidnapper wait four days to make a ransom demand? Something else is going on here, Eric. I can feel it in my bones."

40

"And you think the guy in the sketch you released is behind it?"

"Oh, he's involved all right. He was the last person Doyle was seen with. But he's just a little guy compared to Doyle. Abducting somebody twice your size is quite a feat. Of course, he could have tricked him into leaving the bar with him — maybe even drugged him — but how do you stop Doyle from beating the crap out of you after he wakes up? Unless, of course, you kill him right off. But if Doyle is dead, why haven't we found his body? And now this ransom demand. So, if Doyle is still alive, and the guy in the sketch is the kidnapper, then how is this little guy holding on to him?"

On the other end of the line, Maddox was quiet for almost a minute. "Okay, Rich, tell you what," he finally said. "Your intuition has paid off too many times for me to ignore it. Let's do this. You send us over the original ransom note, and copies of whatever else you have. My guys will proceed as if this is a kidnapping, and that what the kidnapper is interested in is a payday. You go ahead and investigate whatever other angle you come up with. And we keep each other informed. Deal?"

"Deal!"

Chapter 15

As soon as Doyle went missing, the Marauders organization began to plan around the distinct possibility that he would not be available for the following Sunday's game against Las Vegas. There was no way Nolan would be able to play; the team doctor said his collarbone was healing nicely, but that his original prognosis — that Nolan would be out for the rest of the season — was still valid.

The third-string quarterback, a highly touted youngster out of Utah State picked up in free agency after the draft, named Joe Coulter, had seen very little playing time. Coach Ferguson had put him into games only when Bobby Doyle had put the team so far ahead that the Marauders would win, regardless of how badly Coulter might screw up. On those occasions, Coulter, while no Bobby Doyle, managed to hold his own, and in one game, had actually led the team to a late touchdown.

When questioned by the media, Ferguson's official statement was "In the event Bobby Doyle is still missing by next Sunday's game, I have every confidence in Joe Coulter at the quarterback position."

In reality, Ferguson and the team management were scrambling. They were looking hard to find some reasonably talented, seasoned, quarterback to back up Coulter in the event that the untried rookie fell flat on his face in his first start. They eventually managed to locate Sam McArdle, who had played in the league for nine seasons, but who had been released by the New England organization at the start of the season because of salary caps. He had quarterbacked for three different teams in his tenure, and had played for New England the last two seasons. McArdle was deemed to be competent at the position, but conservative, and hardly a standout. If he wasn't a star, then at least he was a good technician. He should, Ferguson reasoned, do well enough to win games, provided he was given the protection of a good offensive line, and he stayed in the pocket. And the Marauders had a *great* offensive line!

McArdle reported to the team that Friday. He had, of course, no time whatever to learn the team's playing system, but he was, after all, only supposed to be a backup for Coulter. Meanwhile, Ferguson prayed for a miracle: Bobby Doyle's quick return to the team.

That same Friday, Alvaro Gomez gave notice at Elegance Yachts.

Chapter 16

"But that's crazy," Doyle said, to his captor, genuinely in anguish. *I'm at the mercy of a complete nut job! How can I convince this guy that I had nothing to do with his sister's suicide or did something to cause his old man's heart attack?*

"Look," Doyle continued, "Alvaro is it? I never even met your sister, much less got her pregnant. But even if I did, how could I be responsible for her killing herself, or for your father's heart attack? Look, man, this is all a big mistake. Just let me out of here and we'll forget the whole thing, okay?"

"No mistake, Bobby, no mistake at all. Elaina may have been foolish, but she was far from stupid. She said she had sex only once, with one man—*you*—and Elaina never lied. Not once in her entire life. She was a good girl, a fine woman, until you ruined her."

"I never," Doyle responded. "Sure, I get around, and I'm only human. I've been with plenty of girls, but I'm always careful. I *always* use protection. *Always.* So even if I did go with your sister once—and I'm not sayin' I did—then I never got her pregnant. Couldn't have."

"Protection? Don't you know nothin', Doyle? Protection? No 'protection' is a hundred percent! And what's to say you weren't drunk out of your gourd at the time and just forgot? Elaina said you both had plenty to drink that night!"

And Bobby Doyle had to admit to himself that that, yeah, sometimes, however rarely, protection *does* fail, and, yeah, he frequently had sex when both he and the woman were *very* drunk.

"And when she came to you, told you she was pregnant, what did you tell her? 'Get rid of it!' you said. You went to Catholic school, and I read where you're supposed to be

Catholic. What kind of a good Catholic tells a woman to go and do something like that? No kind!"

Oh shit! That *girl!* Doyle thought. And the whole incident came flooding back to him. *Now* he remembered Elaina Gomez. And he remembered how certain he was, at the time, that she had been lying and was just trying to take advantage of him. And he did tell her she should maybe get an abortion—something he never would have said if he had actually thought for one second that the child might really be his. But then, Alvaro Gomez's implication was pretty well right on—he really *was not* a very good Catholic. But there was no way he would have ever let *any* woman abort *his* child! And that did not have much to do with his being a Catholic.

Chapter 17

The next thing Vitelli did was delve into Bobby Doyle's background to see if there might have been another reason — aside from greed — for his abduction.

Vitelli was limited when it came to electronic skills; he had Johnny Fowler do a web search on Doyle and to what he could dig up. He was a bit surprised when, after about ninety minutes, Johnny handed him a sheaf of printouts. "Damn," he said, "this thing is thicker than his case file!"

"Lotta stuff out there on the Internet and in the public domain," Johnny countered. "Someday, you might wanna check it out yourself."

"Might just do that," Vitelli responded. *If I ever want to figure out how.* To say that Vitelli was electronically challenged would be a kindness. A troglodyte, he was still trying to figure out how to use the smart phone he had bought six months earlier. Vitelli was actually perversely proud of his unwillingness to acquire the necessary skills to master any electronic device.

"If you ever want to find out what there is on you out on the web, just type your name into Google," Johnny said, smiling. It was almost as if he could read Vitelli's thoughts.

"Right," Vitelli said, and turned his attention to the handful of papers Johnny had given him.

JOHNNY HAD PUT EVERYTHING into chronological order, and Vitelli just scanned through most of the articles describing Doyle's prowess as a high school athlete. What Vitelli did note was that Doyle was not just a phenom on the high school gridiron, he had also excelled at track and basketball.

Doyle then got an athletic scholarship to Boston College. There followed celebratory articles on his success as the BC quarterback, most saying the team's record could have been so much better had the rest of the squad played up to Doyle's skill level.

Then Vitelli saw the article concerning the paternity suit filed against Doyle in his Junior year at BC. The article was practically void of any details, mentioning only that the plaintiff was one Elaina Gomez, also a Boston College student. The article also said that Ms. Gomez had refused to issue a statement, while Bobby had forcefully maintained his innocence. The administration at BC had also refused to make a statement, citing a refusal to comment on "ongoing litigation." Vitelli set that report aside and went on through the rest of the papers. There was, he noted, no further mention of the lawsuit in the rest of the packet.

The remaining papers described the Boston College Eagles' failure to win barely more than half of their conference games in two of Doyle's four years at quarterback, and to win only one of the two bowl games they played: the one played in Doyle's Senior year.

Then there was an article praising the Marauders for picking up Doyle in the eleventh round of the draft. The writer correctly predicted that Doyle would truly shine, once he got the chance to prove himself in the big leagues. And the remaining articles went on to describe how he had done exactly that.

Having gone through the handful of papers, Vitelli picked back up the one article he had set aside, and resolved to find out more about this paternity suit, and perhaps find out why nothing had come of it. He handed the article to Johnny Fowler and said, "Do your computer thing, and see what you can dig up about this in the public record, will you?"

"You know the Community College has computer courses for the electronically challenged, don't you, Rich?" he said, grinning, taking the article from him. Vitelli turned away, pretending to ignore him.

On Friday morning, Johnny Fowler handed Vitelli a copy of the paternity suit filed against Bobby Doyle; it had been sent to him electronically from the Boston Municipal Court.

There was also a Metro Police report that Bobby Doyle's black Cadillac Escalade had been found out by the railyards, parked in a vacant lot next to an empty storefront. It was up on crude blocks and had been stripped clean.

Chapter 18

Viktor Korborov put out the word to all his minions on the street. They were to use the sketch the police had given to the media, and ask around, find out if anybody knew this guy, or anything else anyone might know about Bobby Doyle's disappearance. Then they were to get back to him quickly with anything they found out. Reports did indeed come back to him quickly.

Two of those reports that came back interested him in particular: one from his man who sold drugs to the well-to-do living in East Lakeside. At a bar there, a place called Half Time, a man named Arnold Schuster was bragging about how he was working with the police to find Doyle, and how he had provided some vital information that could help them find him. Schuster was saying he had been practically assured by the police that he would be collecting that "fifty large" reward any time now. "Bring this Schuster person in," Korborov ordered. "I would like to talk to him."

The second report that came in was about an old homeless man, one Horace Blake, a Desert Storm veteran, who lived by the railyards. He had seen a black Escalade drive up onto a vacant lot near the place where he had set up his cardboard-box shelter. He observed the driver pull his passenger from the Escalade and walk him over to an older-model Japanese car, get the guy inside, and then drive off. He also said the local gangbangers came and stripped the Escalade clean before dawn, and when the cops finally came around to impound it, he heard, somewhere, that the Escalade had belonged to some famous football player. Korborov's man said he tried to get more information from the homeless guy, Horace Blake, but failed. "He was pretty spacey," he reported, "and when I pushed him on the make and model of the second car he just said 'gray, I think,' and then asked if I had some change."

"That is probably a dead end," Korborov concluded, "but bring the old man in also. If he is living on the street, he should not be hard to find again."

Chapter 19

The lawyer for the plaintiff in the paternity suit filing was listed as one "Anthony J. Reilly, Esq." Vitelli had Johnny Fowler look him up on his computer and get a phone number.

When Vitelli dialed the number, a nasal-voiced woman answered. He identified himself, and asked to speak to Mr. Reilly about an urgent police matter. But the woman said that she was sorry, but Mr. Reilly was in court all that morning, and wouldn't be back in the office until around two o'clock that afternoon. *One o'clock our time,* thought Vitelli, who then said, "Please tell Mr. Reilly that, again, this is urgent police business, and that I need to speak to him." Vitelli left his phone number, but figured that if Reilly was the typical lawyer, and that since he was not an existing or potential client, he would never return his call; no matter, Vitelli had *his* number, and he would call again himself after one o'clock.

So Vitelli was pleasantly surprised when Anthony J. Reilly actually *did* return his call at 1:05 that afternoon.

"Yessir, Mr. Reilly, thank you for returning my call. I really do appreciate it."

"No matter. Call me Tony, if you would, Detective. Now how can I help you?"

"Well, Tony," Vitelli began, and asked if Reilly could recall the circumstances surrounding the Gomez vs. Doyle paternity suit filing.

"Sure thing, Detective. Remember it well. Never actually spoke more than two or three sentences with the Gomez woman herself, though. It was her brother, Alvaro, who was actually pushing the suit. He paid for the filing."

"Let me guess. Hispanic, maybe a hundred seventy pounds, around five-eight or nine, brown eyes, black hair, long, maybe in a pigtail, thin moustache, gold earring in his left ear?"

Reilly laughed. "Yep! That sounds like Alvaro Gomez to a T. What's this about, anyway, Detective? What's this guy Gomez done? Look, I can put two and two together here. You think he had something to do with Bobby Doyle's going missing?"

"Too early to say, Tony. We're just exploring the possibilities, is all. Apparently, our Mr. Gomez had every reason to be upset with Bobby Doyle. How about you fill me in on all the details behind this paternity suit?"

Reilly went over the details related to the filing. He said that Alvaro explained the circumstances surrounding Elaina's pregnancy. "So, I advised Gomez that Elaina should file a paternity suit against Doyle, and force him to pay her medical expenses, pay child support after the baby was born, and for the next eighteen years thereafter. I explained that, if Doyle denied any responsibility, then paternity was really easy to determine after the baby was born, providing the child's DNA matched up with Doyle's. Gomez seemed to think that that would be no problem. He was obviously dead certain that the child was Doyle's."

He ended with "Of course you know the suit was eventually dropped. Reason was, the poor woman lost the baby, or that, at least, was the reason Gomez gave for firing me. Seems the child died *in utero,* and the doctors said she had to carry it to term anyway. It would have been stillborn."

"Would have been?"

"Yeah. She ended up killing herself."

"Wow! Poor woman. And Alvaro Gomez's reaction?"

"Well, all I can say for sure was that he called and canceled my retainer. Since the woman and child were now both deceased, I went ahead and withdrew the suit. Never spoke to Gomez after that. 'Fraid that's all I can tell you about the matter, Detective."

"And it was plenty. You've been a big help, Tony." *And you've given me a motive for Alvaro Gomez wanting to abduct Bobby Doyle!*

"Glad to have been a help. Please call on me again, Detective Vitelli, if I can be of any further assistance."

"I will, Tony, and thank you! I mean that."

"My pleasure."

Chapter 20

Bobby hated it when Gomez left him alone, which was most of the time. He had tried yelling his head off several times, maybe attract some attention, but to no avail. Gomez had been right about that.

No way to tell time. It could be night or day. All I can see is that single stinking light that barely lets me see anything and never goes out, Doyle mused. And while he hated Gomez for what he had done to him, for threatening to kill him, he still felt a strange longing to see him again. Gomez was, after all, his only contact with the world outside his cage and this enclosed room.

In an effort to pass the time, and to get his mind off food, he turned to calisthenics: trunk twists, push-ups, sit-ups, planks, lunges, running in place. He was even able to do some modified pull-ups using the bars on the ceiling, pulling himself up until the top of his head touched the other bars. He was even able to do some modified jumping jacks, if he allowed for the low overhead. All the exercises helped him to somewhat maintain his body, while counting reps helped calm his mind.

Eventually, his captor did show up, and Doyle cursed the fact that he was actually glad to see him.

"Miss me, Doyle?" Gomez taunted. "Have you been examining your conscience? Are you sorry for your sins?" Gomez looked over at his prisoner, envying him for his superlative body, his ebony good looks, unmarred even by a three-day beard; it was easy to see what Elaina saw in him.

Doyle kept his own counsel. This man had control of his life, now, and, although a few choice retorts had come immediately to mind, he refrained from voicing them. "You look different, Al," he finally said.

"Yep, a haircut, lost my moustache, and took out my earring. Seems someone from the bar we both patronized last Sunday had enough moxie to have the cops draw a reasonable likeness of me. Not exact—made my face look too skinny—but close enough. Saw the sketch on TV, and decided I needed to change my image!"

So, at least the cops know someone kidnapped me, Doyle realized.

"Here," Gomez said, "I brought us both something to eat. Papa John's pizza—pepperoni with extra cheese." He tore the lid off the box, put half the pizza on it, and placed it in the pass-through. Doyle had no idea how long it had been since he ate last, but he knew he was really hungry, and tucked in to his half of the pie.

"Slow down, Bobby, you'll die of indigestion first, and then I'll never get to kill you."

Not funny, Doyle thought, still maintaining his silence, *but there's no telling what this maniac is capable of.*

"Not talking much, eh? Well, that's all right, my friend. You'll squeal loudly enough when the time comes."

"Where do you go when you're not here?" Doyle finally asked.

"Ah! He speaks! Where do you *think* I go? Some of us can't make a living by playing games, you know. We actually have to work. I go to work—or at least I *went* to work. I just quit. What else?"

"What do you do, or what *did* you do?"

"Look around you, and you can see what I do. I'm a welder. And I'm damn good at it. But you know that. You've tested those bars, I know you have. That cage would hold a small elephant."

Actually, Doyle had not tested the bars. It was obvious to him when he first laid eyes on them, from the thickness of the steel, and the spacing of the welds, that even Arnold

Schwarzenegger could not have budged them in his heyday. "Yeah," he finally said, "it is built well."

And Gomez chuckled. "Well, indeed. You ain't goin' nowhere. And when you do leave that cage, it will be because I'll be dragging your body out to bury it."

"How can you say that?" Doyle responded. "Even if I did do what you said, and was in some way responsible for your sister's and your father's deaths, how could you even do that, Al? Kill somebody in cold blood?"

"*Some* way responsible? *Some* way? No, Doyle you are just as responsible as if you had fed Elaina those pills yourself! And in the same way you killed my Papi. He is dead because of the grief *you* caused. And for those things, you will pay."

And for that, Doyle had no answer.

Chapter 21

Viktor Korborov's place of business was on the outskirts of the city, well to the east, and well north of the more plush and expensive places where the city's elite built their homes. He often thought that, given the nature of his various enterprises, a more centrally located headquarters might have been a better choice, but Viktor liked it where he was. It was an old corporate headquarters building, one that had been abandoned years ago when the corporation went bust. The upper-level offices had been refurbished for his personal needs, and it was the place Korborov called home. The lower levels were used to run his various enterprises, and the lowest level, the basement, which the corporation had used for in-house parking and storage, was where he was now headed.

After his man Vasyli had softened him up a little bit, Viktor Korborov decided it was time he interviewed Arnold Schuster personally.

He had interviewed that old homeless man earlier, and after some of Vasyli's "softening" and an interrogation, he had determined that the man had nothing to say that would add anything to what he already knew, so Viktor ordered his disposal. Now he turned his attention to Arnold Schuster.

In the building's basement, Korborov found Schuster naked, bloodied, and tied to a chair. His left eye was swollen almost shut, the right eye the same, but not quite as badly. His tormentor, a burly, heavyset man, stood next to the chair. The man looked something like Mr. Clean from the soap ads, but without the inviting smile. This was Vasyli.

"Ah, Vasyli," Korborov addressed him in Russian, "You have been working hard. I see your fists are all bleeding from working with our guests. You really should wear gloves or something, protect those delicate knuckles."

Vasyli grinned at his boss. "I broke the old man's teeth, and I cut my knuckles on the stumps," he said. Then Korborov focused his attention on Arnold Schuster.

"Well, Mr. Schuster," Korborov began, now in his accented English, "I trust Vasyli, here, has been taking good care of you. How are you enjoying our little get-together so far?"

"Why are you doing this?" Schuster replied. "I've already told you people everything I know."

"Oh, Arnold, I am sure you think you have. What I need you to tell me are the things you do not even know you know." He nodded to Vasyli, saying something to him in Russian, who, in turn, bent Schuster's left ring finger back past beyond the breaking point. Schuster screamed in pain and passed out. Another nod, more Russian, and a bucket of ice-cold water was sloshed over the poor man, the shock quickly bringing Schuster back to consciousness.

"You see, *mal'chik*, it is me who asks the questions, not you. Now, do you understand that, or do you need Vasyli, here, to give you some more encouragement?"

"No, sir, please no!" the broken man replied.

"Good. So now we understand each other. That is important, no?"

"Yes, sir."

"That's what I like to see." Korborov produced a photocopy of the police sketch produced from Schuster's description. He held it out in front of Schuster's still-good eye. "Now, this is a picture of the man you say you saw with Bobby Doyle, is it?"

"Yes, sir."

"Good. But this is just a face, no? What else can you tell me about this man? How tall was he?"

62

"About your height, maybe a few inches shorter."

Kerborov did some quick math in his head. "So, about one hundred seventy centimeters, then. I will never understand why you Americans refuse to measure things the way the rest of the world does!" He smiled. "But that is another matter altogether. His complexion. Fair? Dark? In-between?"

"Not fair, more dark, darker than me. You know, Latin, Hispanic."

"Good. His speech, any accent?"

"Yeah, but not Hispanic. Boston. Like Kennedy, maybe."

"Kennedy?"

"John Kennedy. The President, from recordings back in the sixties."

"Ah yes, him. And when this man and Bobby Doyle were speaking, how did they call each other?"

"Call? Please, I don't understand!"

"What names did they use for each other when they spoke?"

"He called Doyle 'Bobby' and Doyle called him 'Al.' "

"Al. Only Al? Not Alan or Alex, maybe?"

"No, just Al."

"And how did he smell?"

"Smell? I didn't notice that he smelled any particular way."

"No cologne? No strong body odor?"

"No, none of those."

"And what were they talking about?"

"Mostly they talked about their old neighborhood, back in Boston. The guy told Bobby he just moved here from there."

"What old neighborhood?"

"Roxbury. I remember. They were both from Roxbury!"

"Did he say where he went to school there?"

"Yeah! He said he went to trade school."

"Did he say where he worked?"

"No. Please! Mostly they talked about Bobby—what Bobby did up there, where Bobby went to school, about the old neighborhood, and about football. They talked mostly about football. And about the Marauders' chances of getting to the league championship game."

"Did he ever mention what *he* did for a living?"

Schuster thought. "Yeah. He did. He said he was a welder."

"Excellent. See how much you knew that you did not know it? Thank you, Mr. Schuster!"

With that, Korborov spoke something in Russian to Vasyli again, turned, and left the room.

THE NEXT MORNING, SATURDAY, the bodies of Arnold Schuster and Horace Blake were found in the same vacant lot where Bobby Doyle's Escalade had been found, also stripped and abandoned.

The coroner's preliminary report said that Blake had died several hours before Schuster, almost certainly from the beating he had received. Schuster had a plastic bag over his head, and had most likely suffocated to death. Once the crime scene had been cleared, Vitelli had Captain Palmer order that both bodies be placed at the beginning of the queue for autopsy at the Metro Police mortuary.

The media had a field day. The fact that Schuster was the one who had come forward with information about Bobby Doyle's abduction, set off a firestorm of speculation. Some outlets went so far as to suggest that some kind of conspiracy was in play. The local media questioned the effectiveness of law enforcement in the city; some went as far as to call for the resignation of the mayor and police commissioner. But, mostly, the biggest concern was how badly the Marauders might perform on Sunday, considering the absence of their star quarterback.

Meanwhile, Korborov put feelers out all over the city, checking metal working operations, machine shops, and welding suppliers—any business that might employ welders. One welder in particular was sought: a five-foot-seven Hispanic male called "Al."

Chapter 22

"So," Maddox said on the telephone, "you think you found the motive behind Doyle's kidnapping?"

"I do," Vitelli answered, "and I don't think it has anything to do with a ransom. I think this thing is personal between Bobby and the guy that abducted him. And I think that guy is Alvaro Gomez."

"And if you're right — and I'm not saying that you are — what do you think the chances are of Doyle's still being alive?"

"That depends. I'm betting Gomez had nothing to do with the killing of Arnold Schuster or that homeless veteran, Horace Blake. I'm thinking that if Doyle were dead already, we'd have found the body. And I don't think that Alvaro Gomez is a killer. At least not yet, he isn't. Nothing from what I've been able to glean about his past would suggest that he's capable of murder. But I do think he has Doyle holed up somewhere, and the he's working up his courage to do just that!"

"Yeah. The plastic bag thing actually sounds like the Russian mob — that's one of their favorite execution methods. But if the Russians aren't the actual kidnappers, then what they have to do with any of this escapes me. Okay, so if your guy Gomez didn't off Schuster and Blake, who did?"

"Somebody else, apparently. Maybe even your Russians. Somebody who doesn't know where Doyle is, but is just as interested to find him as we are. But if it *is* the Russian mob, then they're holding a kind of an investigation parallel to our own. But whoever it is, Russians or not, it *is* certain that that somebody isn't the least bit reticent about committing murder."

"And if Gomez isn't interested in holding Doyle for ransom, then this other interested party is. I get it. Despite the chintzy reward they offered, I should think the Marauders would be willing pay millions to get Doyle back."

"Exactly. We need to find Doyle before these other people do, or before Gomez murders him."

"This guy Gomez. What about his past? What have you found out?"

"Nothing spectacular. Brought up in a Puerto Rican family. Mother still living in Boston, father recently deceased, two siblings — both girls. An older one, married, Juana Vargas, who the mother now lives with, and a younger one, Elaina, now also deceased."

Vitelli then went on to describe what he had learned about the events that led up to the paternity suit being filed against Bobby Doyle, and the reasons behind its subsequent withdrawal.

"So, you think this is about this kid Alvaro Gomez getting back at Doyle," Maddox said.

"I do. I think Gomez blames Doyle for his sister's suicide and his father's heart attack."

"And his description fits the perp sketch your guy made?"

"It has to, or at least be reasonably close. I did give Schuster's verbal description to the lawyer, Anthony Reilly, in Boston, and he said it fit Alvaro Gomez 'to a T.' Never thought to follow up with the sketch, though. I'll have Johnny send him one, just to confirm."

"You do that. But, anyway, I've got to admit everything you just said makes sense, and it's very likely that this Alvaro Gomez is good for the abduction, anyway."

"I agree," Vitalli said. "But the Schuster and Blake killings, if Gomez isn't good for them, then who is?"

"I'm thinking it's that other player out there," Maddox opined. "Bobby Doyle alive is worth millions. Somebody out there wants to find Doyle for themselves and have a *really* good payday."

"And you like the Russian mob for it"

"I do. And the more I think about it, the more the Schuster and Blake murders are Viktor Korborov's style exactly. They found out everything they knew and then made sure nobody else ever will."

"From what I've heard about the Russians, that sounds about right. Okay. Changing the subject, anything back on those ransom demands?"

"Nothing at all came back on the first and last one. The middle guy called back on schedule, and set up a drop point. The Marauders went ahead — against our advice, mind you — assembled the money, and dropped it off as directed. But the only folks who ever showed up were a TV reporter and her camera crew. Said they got a call telling them exactly when and where the drop was. We think the whole thing was a setup. Some idiot out there thinks he's a comedian."

"Sounds about right," Vitelli agreed. "So, Eric, aside from trying to find this Alvaro Gomez, what can you do for me about seeing what more your people can find out in Boston?"

"Well, I can certainly have somebody from the Boston office interview the mother and get a tap on her phone, just in case this Alvaro character calls. Maybe even interview that lawyer, Reilly. Check out the schools, too, maybe."

"All good. Let me know as soon as you find out anything. The last thing we want is to give this guy enough time to screw up enough courage to off Doyle."

"Right. So, Vitelli where to next?"

"See what more I can dig up on Gomez—anything that might help us find him, and hopefully lead us to Doyle alive and well."

"Yeah, that sounds good, Rich," Maddox agreed.

"Seriously, Eric, we find Doyle dead, in a vacant lot somewhere like Schuster and that other poor guy, then we'll have both failed at our jobs. I don't want that to happen."

And Maddox had nothing to add to that.

Chapter 23

Sunday morning Vitelli got up early, fed the cats, and went for a run in the neighborhood. It would soon turn *very* cold in the city, and a blast of bitter winter weather was the usual unwelcome visitor this time of year, a foretaste of winter misery—but not this morning. The autumn air was crisp, and the day bright and sunny. Unlike during his weekday runs, there was little vehicular traffic to contend with, and he got his five miles in fairly quickly.

After a fast shower, Vitelli dressed and headed off to church at St. Anslem's. The church was one of the oldest in the city, and had been built in the Gothic style, the nave in the form of a cross. The vaulted ceilings were high, but the requisite faux marble columns restricted the view of the altar from many sections of the pews. Vitelli liked the richly decorated church; the ornate *baldacchino* over the altar was unusual for a parish church. The beauty of the place was a comfort, and made him feel that if God dwelt anywhere, he certainly dwelt there.

The ten o'clock Mass was in English, and was well attended. The church was full, and even those sections of the pews with restricted vision were in use. The gospel was from Matthew, the one about the beatitudes: "Blessed be the . . ." and so forth. Vitelli never quite got what all that was about, but felt maybe he should.

After Mass, St. Anselm's served doughnuts and coffee. Vitelli knew he shouldn't, but the honey glazed goodies were calling him, and he couldn't resist. *Don't know why I bothered to get up and run, if I'm going to eat this crap,* he chastised himself. But he sucked down the doughnut anyway.

"Hi, I'm Pam." A throaty female voice, accompanied by a tap on the shoulder. Vitelli turned and saw a vision in her

Sunday best—flowing yellow print—almost as tall as he was. He would later describe her face to himself as handsome, rather than pretty. Oval face, clear skin, straight slim nose, bright eyes the color of dark, polished walnut, framed in auburn hair, cut short and business-like. Trim, healthy, athletic figure.

"Rich," he replied. Caught unaware, he didn't add his usual lame joke "my name, not my financial condition."

"Well, Rich," she said, "you look like you might be over thirty and unattached. Are you?"

"I am," he acknowledged, "well over thirty, and a widower."

"Ah," she said. "Same here, but, in my case, a widow. Look, the parish has an over-thirty singles group. We meet on Wednesday evenings, usually for a casual dinner and few beers. How's about joining us this coming Wednesday? We're meeting in the back room at O'Toole's. Could be fun!"

"I might just do that," Vitelli answered. "Will you be there?"

"I will," and a smile lit up her face.

"Pam," a voice came out from the crowd at Vitelli's left, attached to a tall, slim, man with greying temples. "We'd better go, if we're going to join the others for brunch," he said.

"In a minute, John," Pam answered. Then, to Vitelli: "Join us? It's only just down the street at Ham 'n' Goody's."

"Uh . . . can't. Not this morning. But thanks," he said, not quite understanding his own reason for refusing, because he really wanted to go.

"Okay, then," she said. "See you Wednesday, maybe?"

"Yeah, maybe," he replied, and she disappeared off into the crowd with the man with the greying temples.

SUNDAY AFTERNOON'S GAME IN Cincinnati wasn't quite an unmitigated disaster, but close to it. The weather was perfect, sunny and cool, and the partisan crowd in the stadium smelled blood. The Cincinnati team was 5-3, going into the game, and the Marauders under Bobby Doyle should have put them away with little trouble. But Bobby Doyle was still missing, the Marauders weren't the same team without him, and the Cincinnati fans knew it.

Vitelli was home alone and watched the game on TV. The pre-game show was more about Bobby Doyle having gone missing, and the host's speculations on what had happened to him. Only in passing, did he bother to note that Coach Ferguson would most likely be starting the game with the rookie Joe Coulter at quarterback.

Coulter started out well, Vitell thought, and actually played competently enough in the first half. But the Cincinnati quarterback was on fire, as the contagion spread to the rest of his team; at the half, Cincinnati was up by three scores, 24-7.

Midway through the third quarter, after the Cincinnati defense sacked Coulter for the fifth time, the team doctor pulled him from the game when he could not pass the concussion protocol. By then, the opposition was up 31-10. Ferguson had no choice but to put Sam McArdle in.

For someone completely new to the Marauders' playing system, Vitelli judged McArdle's performance as amazing. McArdle led the team to two more touchdowns before they fell apart in the closing minutes of the fourth quarter, when Cincinnati scored three times inside of eight minutes: one a ninety-eight-yard punt return to the Marauders' end zone. In the end, the score was Cincinnati 45, the Marauders 24. The Marauders had gone down in flames.

Vitelli had another frozen dinner, a Semple beer, and then watched a western shoot-'em-up on Prime; Tristan and Isolde were fast asleep beside him on the couch.

Chapter 24

Monday morning, Vitelli placed another call to Anthony J. Reilly, Esq., in Boston and was lucky enough to find hm in his office.

"Yes, Detective, what more can I do for you?"

"Checking up on the sketch of the 'person of interest' I sent you."

"Face a little too narrow, but it's close enough. That's Alvaro Gomez all right."

"Good. We're doing our best to try and locate where in the city Gomez might be holed up. I need anything you can tell me that might give me a clue as to where to start looking."

"Not sure how I can help you with that."

"How about this angle. You said Alvaro paid for his sister's filing expenses, right?"

"I did."

"Okay, how'd he pay? Check, credit card?"

"Check. I don't do credit cards. I can check back and see what bank his checks were drawn on."

"That would certainly help."

"And something else I just thought of," Reilly volunteered, "I also ran a credit check on Gomez. Just to be sure he was good for my fees."

"You do that with all your clients?"

"Not all the time, no. But I do when the client balks when I ask for a retainer, and Gomez did. A lot of new clients do. Can't blame them, really, they don't know any more about me than I know about them."

"Okay, can you tell me what you found out?"

"Better than that. Send me a request on your police letterhead, and I'll email you the report itself."

"Okay, consider the letter on its way. Got a fax number?"

"A fax number? You people still use fax machines?"

"Uh, I think so. How else do I get the request letter up to you quickly?"

"Email me of course." And Reilly gave him his email address.

"Yeah. Okay. I'll have my guy get right on that," a sheepish Vitelli answered.

That afternoon, Johnny Fowler handed Vitelli an Experian credit report for one Alvaro Gomez.

Chapter 25

"So, Viktor, what news do you have for me? I can see you've been busy." It was Monday afternoon, and Anubis Cline spoke into the phone on his secure line.

"We have. Mr. Schuster was very helpful before his unfortunate demise," Korborov replied. "We now have a line on the man who abducted your football player. He is Alvaro Gomez, and he has worked at Elegance Yachts. His former employer has been most helpful in providing information."

"I can imagine," Cline said.

"Gomez worked there as recently as last Friday, when he gave notice. The only address they had for him was a P.O. box for the post office on Western Avenue. We will grab him if and when he shows up to collect his mail. My men will be waiting for him."

"Excellent."

"If Bobby Doyle is still alive, we will find him."

"I'm counting on you, Viktor."

Chapter 26

Using the credit report that Anthony Reilly had provided, Vitelli got on the phone again, this time to Gomez's former employer, Bath Iron Works in Bath, Maine. After listening to the robotic answering system go through its paces, including a series of numerical choices in which he had no interest, he was finally given the option of speaking to an operator by dialing "O." He dialed "O."

"General Dynamics Bath Iron Works Shipyard," a female with a Downeast accent answered. "How may I direct your call?"

"Personnel, please."

Without acknowledging the directive, the operator switched him to another line. Vitelli knew this only because he heard the phone ringing at the other end. And it rang and rang, until it clicked, and a female voice, followed by yet another robotic voice, answered, " 'Sarah Wilkins, Human Resources,' is not available. Please leave your name and number and a brief message, and 'Sarah' will get back to you as soon as possible."

"This is Detective Richard Vitelli, Metro Police, calling on urgent police business. Please call me back as soon as you can." He left a return phone number.

He had not been in a particularly foul mood when he placed the call, but he was when he hung up the phone. To brighten his mood, he decided it was time for an early lunch.

"I'm gonna grab a hot dog out front, Johnny," Vitelli called out to Detective Sargent Johnny Fowler as he headed to the elevator, toward the vendor who sold his wares on the street out front. "If anyone calls, just call my cell."

Fowler nodded, acknowledging that he had heard and understood Vitelli.

But when Vitelli got out in front of the headquarters building, the Sabrett hot dog vendor was not there. *Perfect,* he thought, *just perfect. That guy and his stand haven't missed a weekday here, rain or shine, in forever.* And, of course, now that he could not satisfy his urge, the urge became a craving. He could almost taste the foot-long, all-beef, kosher-style dog, smothered with a generous helping of fresh sauerkraut, and that delicious, special, tomato-based onion sauce. He even imagined downing it with an ice-cold Semple beer, instead of the usual iced tea he normally had with it at lunch (he was, after all, on duty).

Now, hungry, his craving unsatisfied, Vitelli headed back up to his office in an even fouler mood than when he had left the building. *I eat too much anyway,* he mused. *I could stand to lose a pound or two.*

He was headed to his desk when Johnny Fowler called out to him, "Rich! There you are! You have a call holding on line one." Vitelli nodded at Johnny and hurried to his desk.

"Detective Lieutenant Vitelli," he said into the phone.

"Yes, Detective, this is Sarah Wilkins, Bath Iron Works Human Relations, you called earlier?"

"I did, Ms. Wilkins. A person of interest in an ongoing police investigation was reported to be a former employee at the shipyard. His name is Alvaro Gomez. What can you tell me about him?"

"Just a second, Detective," and Vitelli could hear some clicking sounds as Wilkins accessed her computer. "Here we are, Detective. I can confirm that Alvaro Jaime Gomez was indeed employed here at the shipyard. He worked here at General Dynamics Bath Iron Works for almost three years, until he gave notice last June fourteenth."

"Okay. What position did Mr. Gomez hold?

"I'm afraid, Detective, that all I can tell you is that Mr. Gomez was indeed employed here. Federal law, requires . . ."

"I understand that, Ms. Wilkins, I do. But this is an ongoing police investigation. Surely you can tell me . . ."

"Only what I have told you already, Detective," Ms. Wilkins retorted, obviously getting annoyed. "If you want more information than that, I'm afraid I would have to have a federal court order."

"Yes, Ma'am," Vitelli responded, equally annoyed. "Thank you for returning my call."

"My pleasure, Detective," came the frosty reply.

Vitelli's day had not gotten any brighter.

Vitelli placed a call to Eric Maddox and asked if he could break through the information barrier at Bath Iron Works. Maddox only chuckled and said "I'll see what I can do. You know, Rich, you really ought to dump the Metro Police Department and join the FBI. Life could be so much simpler."

"Yeah, Eric," Vitelli answered, "it might just. But for now, just get me what I need from bath Iron Works."

"Roger that!" was Maddox's reply.

Maddox called back two hours later, and told Vitelli, "Gomez was apparently a model employee at the shipyard. They hired him as an apprentice welder directly after he graduated from Boston Joint Apprentice Training Center. He quickly advanced to, first, Journeyman Welder, and then to Master Welder, all apparently in record time. His attendance record was excellent, and when he gave notice, he left no immediate forwarding address. He did, however, eventually contact the shipyard and give a post office box number address in the city, Western Avenue Station box number 4385, so they could mail him his final check, and his W-2 forms. His emergency contact was one Violetta Sanchez Gomez, with a Boston address and telephone number."

"Good work, Eric. How'd you manage to get all that out of them when they stonewalled me?"

Maddox laughed. "You just didn't ask nicely enough! And it helps if you're FBI, amigo, and a federal judge tells them to cooperate."

"So it would seem."

"I keep telling you, Rich, you're working for the wrong outfit! You need to come over from the dark side."

"Never mind that. I need to get a watch on that P.O. box."

"Already done. Anybody goes near it, we'll know. And they will not get far."

"Good to know. Guess it's too much to ask if he told them who hired him locally."

"I wish."

"Yeah, me too. Still, there can only be so many places that hire master welders."

"Sounds like a job for your man Fowler."

"It does. Poor Johnny's gonna hate me for this."

"Nothing new about that, my friend!"

"Did your guys in Boston interview the mother, check out the schools, yet?"

"Not yet. Though they have set up to interview the mother in the morning."

"Good. Keep me posted, please!"

"Wilco."

Eric was right about one thing: Johnny really was not happy about his new assignment at all.

Chapter 27

Bobby Doyle noticed that Alvaro checked on him more often now than he had at first, when it seemed that he was alone for much longer periods. He asked him why that was.

"Because, Bobby, I told you. I quit my job."

Doyle realized he had indeed told him that. *God help me, I'm getting spacey!* "Why'd you do that—quit your job?"

"'Cause that sketch of me is all over the place. It's not perfect, but it's close enough that my ex-boss would probably see the resemblance. The moustache, the hair, the earring, after all. I figured it was about time for me to leave, before the old guy made the connection."

"What'll you do for money? Don't you need a paycheck?"

"I have enough money to do what I need to do. And if I do run out, then I can just let you starve to death, eh?"

Doyle said nothing. He knew that Gomez reveled in the power he had over him and refused, as much as he could, to encourage him.

"Don't worry, Bobby, I won't let you starve. It would take too long. But when the time comes, you will be begging me to shoot you, and get it over with."

"Look, Alvaro, you can't do that. You're Catholic, right? You murder me and you'll be committing mortal sin—you'll be sending your soul straight to hell."

"Perhaps, Bobby, perhaps. But only after I send *you* straight to hell! What you did was murder too, wasn't it?"

"Yeah, well, I've been thinking about that. About going to hell, I mean. You can't do that, Alvaro. You can't kill me without giving me a chance to confess my sins to a priest. No

Catholic would do that to another Catholic. You gotta let me go to confession."

"I don't gotta let you do nothin'!" Gomez shouted. "You didn't think about that while my little sister was sucking down those pills, or when my Papi was dying of a heart attack! You don't deserve nothin'! Not one damn thing!"

Doyle sensed that the best response to that tirade was no response at all. He maintained his silence as Alvaro stormed out of the room, and into the great beyond behind the slammed door.

BUT WHAT DOYLE HAD just said began to weigh on Alvaro's conscience. A somewhat indifferent Catholic himself, he nonetheless believed in his religion's basic tenets: the forgiveness of sins; the existence of heaven and hell; and that the way one behaved in this life determined how and where one would spend forever in the next.

Killin' the bastard is one thing, Alvaro mused. *He deserves to die for what he did to Elaina and Papi. But nobody deserves to spend all eternity in Hell if he can avoid it. He deserves killing, all right, but I certainly don't want to be the reason Doyle ends up in Hell afterward. Or, then, maybe I'll have to join him there.* He realized, of course, that murdering another human being was a deadly sin, and that the act would condemn his own soul to eternal damnation. But he was also planning on outliving Doyle for a long time, and there would be plenty of time for penance afterwards, when he could wrap his mind about being truly penitent—but only *after* he killed Bobby Doyle.

Yes, there would be plenty of time later for him to regret having killed Doyle, confess his sins to a priest, get absolution, and do whatever penance was necessary after that—anything to keep him from eternal punishment.

Shit! he then realized, *I can kill him all right, that part's easy. But sending him to Hell forever? I can't do that! I gotta find a priest for Doyle to confess to!*

Chapter 28

"There were so many businesses in the city that could employ welders that I would have had to call every one of them and ask if they had hired anyone who fit this guy Gomez's description," Johnny Fowler said. "I would have been on the phone the rest of the week."

"Yeah, but Gomez is a *master welder*. That makes a difference, no?" Vitelli replied.

"No, it is the same difference. So, instead of giving Gomez's description, I call and ask if they hire master welders. Still have to make all those calls, no?"

"I guess. So where are you going with this?"

"Just showing you how smart I am. I figured this Gomez worked up in Maine at Bath Iron Works, right?"

"Correct."

"Maine—government contractor—has to belong to a union, no?"

"Probably." A light went off over Vitelli's head. "Oh, I see! You found out which union Bath has for welders . . ."

"Bingo! Machinists Union. Called the local here. Gomez works at Elegance Yachts. Been there a few months, too, since July. So then I called Elegance Yachts. Spoke to a guy named Ezra Farnsworth, runs the place. Said he was afraid to give me any info over the phone."

"Afraid? Why afraid?"

"He would not say. But it sounds like you need to talk to him, yourself, no? Maybe even pay the place a visit?"

"It does indeed," Vitelli replied, "but I'll try calling him, first," and Johnny flashed a self-satisfied smile. "Good work. as usual, Johnny. I'm gonna ask Parker to double your salary!"

"Fat chance of that," Fowler replied.

Chapter 29

Father William Dale was just four years out of seminary. He had initially served as Assistant Pastor under a seasoned priest in the Diocese, but there was a shortage of priests, and Father William had done well enough at that job to be given a small parish of his own: Stella Maris. It was an urban parish just outside the city's industrial belt, and just two blocks away from St. Justin Martyr Academy, the diocesan girls high school, where Father William also served as school chaplain.

Father William had been at Stella Maris for just over a year, and had yet to take a day off, let alone take a vacation. There were two daily Masses to celebrate: Vigil Mass on Saturday evening, and three more on Sunday (one of those in Spanish). Then there was the weekly Tuesday morning Mass at the high school, and confessions in the church on Saturday afternoon before the Vigil Mass. Throw in an occasional wedding, a funeral, or a baptism, and he barely had a minute to himself. The bishop sent a priest from the chancery to celebrate the two daily Masses on Mondays, so he could have at least one day off, but there was usually some emergency or other that came up on that day anyway: a parishioner in the hospital, a married couple in need of counseling, or even someone coming off the street wanting food, or to go to confession. Father William Dale was a busy man, but he would not have had it any other way—he loved every minute of his busy life.

So, he was not the least bit fazed when a lean young Hispanic man with a Boston accent showed up at the rectory early Monday afternoon, and asked him to hear his confession.

"Bless me, Father, for I have sinned. It's been—I don't know—a couple of years at least since my last confession."

"Welcome back, young man! Go on."

"Look, Father, I've done a lot of stuff I shouldn't have. But it's what I'm planning on doing that I really need to talk to you about." Alvaro Gomez paused, gathering his thoughts, and Father William waited, saying nothing.

"You know about Bobby Doyle, the Marauders' quarterback going missing, right?"

"I do."

"Well, Father, that was me. I did that—kidnapped him." Alvaro looked up at the priest, and saw the incredulous look on his face, the doubt obvious in his blue eyes. "Okay, so you don't believe me."

"I didn't say that."

"You don't have to. It's written all over you. But it's true. Sure, he's twice my size, but I drugged him, got him into my car, and I'm holding him in a steel cage in a warehouse across the city. And I'm going to kill him for what he did to my sister and my father." Alvaro then went on to describe to Father William about how Doyle got his sister pregnant, her subsequent suicide, and his father's heart attack, and how he held Doyle responsible.

"All right," the priest replied, "but certainly you must see that even if all you said is true, and Bobby Doyle truly is responsible for everything that you say he is, that it is just as sinful for you to take revenge. If you did kidnap him and are holding him prisoner . . . if you did all this, my son—"

"Alvaro. My name is Alvaro. Alvaro Gomez."

"Okay, Alvaro, but saying you really did all this—and what you've already done is certainly a serious sin—it pales in comparison to your plan to murder Bobby Doyle. I can give you absolution for what you have done, provided you release him unharmed, but certainly not for what you're planning on doing. Certainly, you have to see that." Father William was beginning to believe that this man *was* exactly who and what he said he was. He recalled the sketch that had been on TV: *A haircut and a shave, and this could be the same person. And he* does *have a pierced left ear!*

"Oh, Father, I really didn't expect you to give me absolution. Not today, anyway. But I still wanted you to hear my confession. That way you can't say anything about what I just told you, right?"

"Well, that *is* true. The seal of confession."

"I figured. The thing is, Father, I'm really going to kill Doyle no matter what. But, say I do it, and am really and truly sorry afterwards, I'm going to have the opportunity at least to go to confession then and not go to Hell when I die. And as much as I hate Doyle for what he did to my family, I don't hate him enough to send him to Hell for all eternity either. He's Catholic, Father, and has asked me to let him go to confession. So that's the whole of it, Father, I want you to come with me and hear Doyle's confession."

"You're serious."

"Deadly serious. If you don't come, Doyle never gets to confess. Then, when I shoot him, he goes straight to Hell."

"Well, not exactly. Not if he's truly sorry for anything he's done and would go to confession if he could."

"Yeah, well maybe. But it's certainly not as sure as actually receiving the sacrament, now, is it?"

"No," the priest agreed, "perhaps it's not."

"Then you'll *have* to come with me."

And that's how Father William found himself, against sound secular judgment, agreeing to go with Alvaro to where he was holding Bobby Doyle prisoner, so he could hear the man's confession.

Chapter 30

Vitelli called Elegance Yachts and asked to speak to Ezra Farnsworth.

"Farnsworth."

"Yes, Mr. Farnsworth, this is Detective Lieutenant Richard Vitelli, Metro Police. If you have a minute, I'd like to talk to you about one of your employees."

"Certainly, Detective. The law limits what I can tell you, but I can give you some information. Which employee?"

"Alvaro Gomez."

"I'm sorry, Detective. I can't tell you anything about him."

"Sure you can. Employment law says you can tell me if he still works there, when he started working there, and, if he left the job, also if he left a forwarding address."

"No. I won't do any of that."

"And why not, sir?'

"I won't, is all." And he hung up.

Vitelli was furious. *Son of a bitch hung up on me!* He called again, this time identifying himself to the person who answered the phone, and asked again to speak to Farnsworth.

"I'm sorry, sir, but Mr. Farnsworth is in a meeting. May I take a message?"

"No, thank you," Vitelli replied. "Never mind," and hung up. He told Johnny he was going to pay Ezra Farnsworth a visit, and drove across town to the shipyard. *This time Farnsworth will answer my questions whether he wants to or not!*

WHEN VITELLI FINALLY DID confront Farnsworth he found a round, frightened little man.

"What exactly is your problem, Mr. Farnsworth?" Vitelli asked.

"They told me they'd come back and kill me if I said anything to anybody about Gomez or about their being here."

"Who did, Mr. Farnsworth?"

"Big Russian guy. Called himself Vasyli. *Big* guy, built like the jolly green giant, except he was pink, and he was not at all jolly. Was here waiting when I opened up the place this morning. First, he asked if Gomez was here, and when I said he wasn't, he asked me when he was due in to work. I told him Gomez had quit. So he says that he needs his forwarding address. I told him I couldn't give him that information, and he started to get really nasty."

"Nasty how?"

"He started yelling at me, pushed me against the wall, and demanded to see Gomez's employment file. When I told him, 'no,' that it was against the law, he grabbed me by the throat and threatened to kill me and then burn the place down unless I gave it up to him. I don't mind telling you he scared the shit out of me."

"I'm sure he did. Then what happened?"

"Long story short, I gave him the file. He took it, and said if I told anyone, he'd come back and finish the job. I think that big bastard would have killed me then and there anyway, but, by then, there were other people in the office, and there would have been too many witnesses he's also have to kill."

"He give you the file back?"

"No, he kept it. So now there *is* no file, Detective, none at all. I know I broke the law by giving it to him, but I had no choice. So now I guess you're going to arrest me?"

"No, Mr. Farnsworth, I'm not going to arrest you. But I do need to know whatever you can remember was in that file."

"Like what?"

"I understand from what you said he no longer works here. When did he work here last?"

"Last Friday. Been here a couple months. Leaves for work at the end of his shift and gives notice. Just like that. Damn shame, too. Gomez was a hell of a good welder—no, he was a *great* welder! I was damn sorry to lose him."

"And when did this Russian goon show up?"

"Told you. First thing this morning. Scared the shit out of me."

"Did Gomez give you a forwarding address?"

"Just a post office box."

"Can you remember it?"

"No, but wait a minute, we mail him his paychecks. Hang on a second, I'll check with my guy." Farnsworth left and returned a few minutes later, handing Vitelli a slip of notepaper. On it was written: P.O. Box 4325, Western Avenue Station.

"Got a phone number for him?" Vitelli asked.

"I'll check with the receptionist. She'll have one." He left and came back again with another slip of paper, this time with a phone number on it.

"One last thing," Vitelli said, "his last paycheck. You say he gave notice Friday. Did you pay him then?"

"No. My bookkeeper tallies up the hours worked, and figures out what each employee is owed for the previous week on Mondays. Has to take out the taxes and the union dues and all that crap, you know. Then she mails out the checks, so they will be going out tonight. Gomez's last check will be in the mail tonight. He could have it in his P.O. Box as early as sometime tomorrow, or Wednesday, latest, I would imagine. I t only has to go across town."

"Right. Thanks, Mr. Farnsworth. If I think of anything else I need, I'll be back in touch."

"Okay, Detective," and then he scowled, and, agitated, he asked, "What if he shows up again, Vasyli, the Russian guy?"

"I seriously doubt he will, sir. With the Russian mob, if they had meant to kill you, you'd be dead already."

"That's not very reassuring!"

"No, I guess not," Vitelli answered with a smile, "Tell you what I can do, I can make sure a black-and-white is parked outside for the next couple of days or so. And make sure a mobile patrol does regular checks on the place, maybe."

"That would be good," Farnsworth answered, but he did not sound very reassured.

Chapter 31

Father William walked out to Alvaro's car and got in the passenger side, noting the vehicle's make, model and color.

"There's a black hood next to you in the seat, Father," Alvaro said. "Put it on, please."

"Is that really necessary, Alvaro?"

"Com'on, Father, you know it is. Same reason I made you leave your watch and cell phone back inside the rectory. Maybe you can't tell the cops what I told you in confession, but you could tell them where I'm holding Bobby Doyle, or at least how to get there from here. You would if you could— you know you would. I'm afraid we don't go nowhere unless you put the hood on."

Reluctantly, Father William donned the hood. It was an effective one, and he could not see a thing with it on. For a while he tried to count the seconds between turns and gage their direction, left or right, but he quickly lost count. Besides, he was sure that Alvaro was purposely driving in circles, just to confuse him. In between a continued effort to talk Gomez out of his vendetta against Doyle, Father William paid attention to traffic noises, and noted that there was less and less outside noise as time passed. He figured that about a half hour or so had passed, when the car stopped, and he heard the sound of an overhead door. He felt a slight bump after the vehicle began to move again. When the car stopped once more, and Alvaro had turned off the engine, he went to take the hood off, but Alvaro stopped him.

"Not yet, Father. Not until we're inside of Doyle's cell. I'll lead the way. It's all level floor between here and there."

Gomez guided Father William to the door of the sound enclosure room and opened it. He opened the door wide, and said "There's a step up, here, Father," and, guiding him up and over the step, then said "Okay, Father, when I close the door, you can take the hood off."

As soon as the door to the enclosure was opened, Father William could smell, even through the hood, the miasma of a body held in confinement over so many days: heavy body odor, and the dank odor of human excrement.

Inside, with the door open wide and held open, Bobby Doyle could, for the first time, get a clear view of the world outside his enclosure. There was, he could see, a far wall, maybe forty yards or so away, covered in some kind of white plastic sheeting, and the floor: flat, polished concrete. *I'm in a room built inside a damn warehouse!* he suddenly realized.

With the hood off, Father William found himself staring at a muscular black man with an unkempt beard, standing inside an intricate steel cage. *Bobby Doyle in the flesh,* he thought, *looking much the worse for wear.*

In turn, Doyle stared at a tall, lean, white man, dressed in clerical garb: Roman collar, black trousers, black suit jacket and shirt front. He had a clean-shaven, handsome face, even-featured, neatly-combed black hair, deep concern expressed in his blue eyes.

"Bobby, this here," Gomez announced, "is Father William. He's here to hear your confession, just like you asked. Make it a good one, Bobby, 'cause it's gonna be your last." Addressing Father William, he said, "I'll leave you to it, Father. Crack open this door and yell when you're ready to leave, and I'll come get you. But don't leave this room without your hood on, or I'll have to kill you—and we both wouldn't want that, now, would we?"

A chill went up Father William's spine at that, because Gomez sounded like he was perfectly serious. Father William said nothing in response. Gomez then smiled, turned, and left the room, closing the door behind him.

Chapter 32

Vitelli called Eric Maddox and told him what he had found out at Elegance Yachts.

"Vasyli, eh? That sounds like one of Viktor Korborov's goons."

"Korborov? So, you really *do* think it's the Russian mob that's working against us, trying to find Doyle."

"Like I said before, that would explain the dead bodies. And if they have the P.O. box number, they will be staking it out just in case Gomez shows up to collect his paycheck. So, I guess it was good I put my guys on it too, 'round-the-clock. Wouldn't want the Russians to get to Gomez before we do."

"No, that wouldn't do at all!"

"Listen, the Boston office did an interview with the mother. And the lawyer. I'll send you over copies of the reports, but they don't tell us very much beyond what we already knew. His mother, for example, is certain her son Alvaro holds Doyle personally responsible for her daughter's suicide and her husband's death. And that he's planning something stupid. She says she hadn't heard from him in weeks. She pleaded with our guy to stop him before he gets himself in some serious trouble."

"Afraid it's a little late for that."

"I guess."

VITELLI SAT ACROSS FROM Captain Parker's desk and brought him up to speed.

"It's for sure that this Alvaro Gomez guy abducted Bobby Doyle. What I can't figure out is what he did with — or is still doing with — Doyle since he grabbed him. He believes he has got every reason in the world for wanting Doyle dead. He obviously blames him for his sister and his father's deaths.

So, he has either figured out a way to hold Doyle prisoner, or Doyle is lying dead somewhere and we just haven't found the body."

"Well, he might just be pumping him up with drugs, to keep him quiet," Parker opined, "and if Doyle's already dead, maybe your dry cleaner lady is back in business, and we'll never find the body, ever."

"Well, I'm pretty sure our 'dry cleaner lady' has left town for good. And if Gomez is keeping Doyle drugged, he can only keep that up for so long before Doyle dies anyway. Let's just hope that if Doyle's still alive, and Gomez has found a way to incarcerate him somehow. Maybe he's working up his nerve before actually killing him."

"Or torturing him, maybe."

"I don't think Gomez would do that, Captain. Not physical torture, anyway. Not if I'm reading him right. But I wouldn't put it past him to put a bullet in Doyle's brain once he worked himself up to it."

"Well, if Doyle *is* still alive," Parker said, "we'll just have to catch Gomez before he does the deed. Or before our Russian friends find him. I saw that the autopsy reports came back on Schuster and Blake. Apparently, before they were killed, they were beaten to a pulp, and by the same person. Each body had two different DNA profiles in the blood that covered them, one belonging to the victim and another one that both bodies shared. That extra DNA has to belong to the person who beat them up, and the medical examiner says that Blake, at least, died from the beating. Schuster died from asphyxiation. He had a plastic bag over his head, poor bastard. But if we ever catch the guy who beat them up, we can positively get him for Blake's murder, if not both."

"Yeah. I seriously doubt our boy Gomez could have done any of that. I make the Russians for both of those murders," Vitelli said.

"It's definitely more their style."

"So how do you see the Russians figure in on all this?" Parker asked.

"Not quite sure. Gotta be about money, though. But it's pretty obvious that they've been conducting an investigation parallel to our own."

"You're referring to our informants showing up dead, of course. And jacking up the owner at the yacht place."

"Exactly. Now that they know as much about Gomez as we do, they will be wanting to find him just as badly."

"Their angle?" Parker asked.

"Again, not sure. What I'm guessing is that they're counting Doyle still being alive and that Gomez can lead them to him. If they do get to Doyle, the Russians are probably figuring on pawning him off to the Marauders organization for a hell of a lot more than the paltry fifty-grand reward money they are offering."

"Sounds about right. Well, we'll just have to get to Gomez before they do. You say the feds got a stakeout going on this P.O. box?"

"Yeah. And it's around-the-clock, since the postal service gives access to P.O. boxes 24/7."

"At least that's not costing *me* money. Let's hope this Gomez guy shows up soon, and the feds get a lead on him before the Russians do."

"Well, thanks to their stealing Gomez's personnel file from Elegance Yachts, the Russians know about the P.O. box too. And you can bet they're also staking it out. That could be some real trouble."

"Yeah, well, maybe the feds are of some use after all."

Chapter 33

"Father, you've got to help me!" Doyle pleaded.

"Other than hear your confession, Bobby, I'm not sure how I can. Your abductor was very clever. He talked me into coming here, and then blindfolded me, so I have no idea whatsoever how to get here, or even where we are."

"Alvaro is clever all right. It wasn't until you came in here, and he held the door open for you, that I could see for the first time that this is really a room inside a much bigger room. The far wall outside the door has some sort of insulation on it, and it's about half a football field away. And this room is soundproof. I know that 'cause I can yell my head off, and nobody outside can hear me. Watch this," and Doyle began shouting out loud. "Al! Come quick! Father needs you! Come right now!"

And nothing happened.

"Point made," Father William said. "So, we're inside a room built inside a much bigger room—like in a gym, or a warehouse, maybe."

"I'm thinking a warehouse, or a factory building. Don't know that a gym would have a concrete floor. But you'll get out of here, because despite what Al might have said, I don't think he has any intention of killing *you*. Now killing *me*, that's another proposition altogether."

"You think he really means to kill you?"

"I do. I think he's just working up the *cojones* to do just that—pardon my French, Father."

"Not a problem, but that's Spanish, not French."

"What?"

"Never mind. Look, I was brought here to hear your confession. Do you want to do that?"

"I do, Father, please."

"Well, then," he said, as he made the sign of the cross in blessing, "please begin."

FATHER WILLIAM CALLED THE Marauders' hot line as soon as he was returned to the rectory, and left a simple message:

"This is Father Willian Dale, Pastor of Stella Maris Catholic parish. Listen, Bobby Doyle is alive. I have met with, and spoken to him, and can describe the place where he is being held prisoner. Call me at . . ." and he left his cell number.

Chapter 34

Anubis Cline retreated back into the world of his own making. He conjured up a vision of his ward, Jael, and saw her so clearly, he could almost reach out and touch her.

I have missed you, my child, to the point of distraction. But now that I have you back, back as my muse and my inspiration, we can once more, together, take on those in the world who would dare to challenge us!

"Abba, I never really left you, you know that. I am always here for you."

So you are, my child. It will be interesting, will it not, to see how the current drama plays out? I am disappointed, of course, that Bobby Doyle has not been found already, dead or alive. The team has suffered one embarrassing loss already. The losses will most likely continue unless Doyle returns alive and well. The longer the situation remains unresolved, the more money I bleed!

"Your man Korborov has identified the man who abducted Doyle, has he not?"

He has. The abductor is Alvaro Gomez. Has this Gomez some real or imagined grievance against Bobby Doyle and is bent on killing him? Or has he simply kidnapped him for ransom? Korborov either doesn't know or wouldn't say.

"If this Gomez wishes to kill Bobb Doyle, he would surely have killed him by now, would he not?

He would, of course! Perhaps the body is just well hidden and has yet to be found. Certainly, if Doyle has been abducted for ransom, this Gomez would have long since asked for money – or was the ransom note the FBI said was fake actually quite real? And, if so, then it was the bungling authorities that frightened him away! Is Doyle still alive? And if he is, will the police, or my Russian friend Korborov find him first?

"I think, Abba, that if Bobby Doyle were dead, his body would have shown up long since. I think he's still alive and somehow being held prisoner. And I think if anyone finds him, it will your man Korborov."

I suspect you are right, my Dear. Any time now, Korborov will call with the news that he has Doyle, and demand a ransom of his own. Then comes decision time. If Korborov is not too greedy, I will have the team pay the ransom. But if he asks too much – more than I can collect from my insurance policy on Doyle – then Doyle becomes more valuable to me dead than alive. Then Korborov can kill or maim Doyle for all I care. Either way, I shall win out.

"Of course, you will, Abba. You always do."

Chapter 35

By the time the skeptical FBI Agent manning the Marauders' hot line passed Father William's message onto Eric Maddox at the main office, it was already Tuesday morning. Maddox immediately called Vitelli.

"Rich, I think we may have a lead. My guy on the hotline thought this was just a crank call, but I called the number the caller—a Catholic priest named Father William Dale—left, and he's for real. Seems he's actually seen and talked to Doyle. He's not sure how much he can help us, other than to confirm that Doyle was very much alive when he saw him."

"Give me the number. I'll set up a meet."

"Already did that. Seems he's celebrating Mass this morning over at the girls high school, Justin Martyr, and he wants us to meet him there. Says the Mass will be over around ten and we can talk to him right after."

"Ten? Okay. I'll meet you there."

"Right. He said the security at the school is pretty tight, but ask for the principal, a Sister Marie Therese Collins, and she'll take us to him."

ST. JUSTIN MARTYR DIOCESAN High School for Girls was an imposing four-story, brick-and-stone edifice in the Edgewood section of the city, not far from downtown. When the school was constructed some seventy years ago, Edgewood was in the country, and the building was surrounded by open fields and farmland. But urban industrial sprawl had turned Edgewood into a less-than-desirable neighborhood, replete with both thriving businesses and abandoned factories and a few rundown housing complexes. The Diocese had purchased a more favorable five-acre site just outside of Westlake, with the intention of relocating the school there, but had yet to raise the funds to proceed with those plans. So, for the interim, the school continued to hold classes in the old neighborhood, but had stepped up security commensurate with their surroundings.

VITELLI MET MADDOX OUTSIDE the entrance to Justin Martyr a little before ten o'clock. He noticed that there was a closed-circuit television (CCTV) camera mounted above the door. Ringing the doorbell brought a female voice out of the speaker next to the door: "Yes, gentlemen, how may I help you?"

"FBI Special Agent Maddox, and Detective Richard Vitelli, Metro Police, here to see the principal, Sister Marie Therese?"

"Yes, sir, you're here to meet with Father William. Sister is expecting you. Please come in." There was an electronic buzz at the door and Maddox and Vitelli entered the building. The interior was all matte-white tile floors, semi-gloss white, painted walls, dark wood trim and high ceilings. A pretty young lady in a school uniform: knee-length blue skirt, white blouse, saddle shoes, and white knee-length socks met them and conducted them down a long corridor to the principal's office.

A smiling round face surrounded by a starched white cowl greeted them. "Good morning, gentlemen, I'm Sister Marie Therese." Then to the young lady who answered the door: "Thank you, Melanie, you may go now."

"Yes, Sister," Melanie answered, and left them.

"Good to meet you, Sister. I'm Special Agent Maddox, and this is Metro Police Detective Richard Vitelli."

"Yes, gentlemen. Father William Dale said to expect you. I have reserved the conference room for your meeting. Besides being pastor at Stella Maris, Father William is the school chaplain, and he says Mass for the student body every

Tuesday morning. Mass should be getting out shortly. We will meet him outside the convocation center. The conference room is just across the hallway from there," she said, and led the way.

The hallway outside the convocation center was empty when they entered it, but it did not stay that way. It quickly filled with noisy girls of all sizes and description, their only commonality being the ubiquitous school uniform present in various stages of wear. Groups of them filed out of the convocation center's two doorways, each led by a nun in a habit identical to that of Sister Marie Therese: There were faces surrounded by starched white cowls; heads covered in black veils; floor-length black dresses, waists cinctured by wooden rosaries.

But one nun was dressed differently. Where all the other sisters were in black, she wore white. And Vitelli found her face instantly familiar. "Sister Marie," Vitelli enquired, "that sister there, the one in white, I believe I know her. Who is she?"

"Ah," said Sister Marie, "that is Sister Lucy Simic. She just joined the order just a year ago. Technically she's still a novice, and won't take her final vows until next year. But she's a whiz in chemistry, and the order is desperate for science teachers, so the mother house sent her to teach here, while she still completes her novitiate. The girls just love her. They say she makes the molecules come alive for them!"

I'll bet she does! Vitelli thought, pretty certain he had just recognized the woman, someone he knew as Leona Barrett, but he said instead, "Well, then, I thought I knew her, but I must be mistaken."

Their conversation was covered by the noise in the hallway, and escaped Maddox's attention.

As quickly as the hallway filled, it emptied. A few minutes later, a tall, lean man, dressed in clerical garb,

Roman-collared black shirt, and sharply-creased black trousers, emerged from the nearest door. Vitelli noted a serious expression, even-featured face, black hair parted on the left, solemn blue eyes. He guessed his age not a day over thirty-five.

Sister Marie Therese made the introductions and conducted them to the conference room, where she left Maddox and Vitelli with Father William.

Chapter 36

Once the trio was comfortably seated at the long, ancient, (but meticulously kept) walnut conference table in the school conference room, Vitelli noticed that the nuns had thoughtfully provided a tray of sugar cookies and pint bottles of water. He surveyed the room: same high, off-white ceilings as in the hallway, matching off-white walls, walnut wainscoting. A tall window gave a clear view of the street below.

Vitelli and Maddox sat opposite Father William, and Maddox began the conversation.

"So, Father, you say you've seen Bobby Doyle alive?"

"I have. He seemed to be in reasonably good condition, although he certainly could have used a shave and a bath."

"Okay. What can you tell us about him and his abductor?" Maddox asked.

"First, gentlemen, let me begin by saying that I am somewhat limited in what I can tell you. I have heard both men's confessions."

"So?" Maddox asked, nonplussed.

Vitelli broke in: "What Father is saying, Eric, is that he's bound by the seal of the confessional."

"The what?"

"The seal of the confessional, Agent Maddox," Father William explained. "Confession is a sacrament, anything confessed to a priest inside confession is private, and may never be revealed or discussed outside the sacrament at any time or for any reason."

"You mean like between a lawyer and his client?"

"Pretty much. Although I don't know if a lawyer can be defrocked if he breaches confidence."

"Pardon me, Father, I'm just an ignorant Baptist, and I never heard of such a thing." Maddox turned to Vitelli, who was smiling. "Okay, Rich, you're Catholic. Is this even legal?"

"I'm pretty sure it is, Eric. But even if it isn't in civil law, I guarantee Father William here will never violate the seal."

"Not even to save a man's life?"

"No, not even then."

"Well, then," Maddox exclaimed, "why are we even here? What *can* you tell us Father?"

"That I saw Bobby Doyle alive yesterday for one thing. That he is being held in a kind of a cage made of steel bars, and that the cage is set up in a soundproofed room. And that the soundproofed room appears to have been constructed inside some larger building, like an abandoned factory, or perhaps a warehouse."

"Well, that's something, I guess," Maddox said, "and valuable information. Can you tell us how to get to this place?"

"I cannot. But that hasn't got anything to do with the sacrament. I was driven there in an old Toyota, a Corolla model, green. But I was made to wear a blindfold—a black hood—*after* I got into the car, and I'm sure I was driven around a bit just to throw me off. It still took about a half hour or so to get there from Stella Maris, though. It was during the day on a Monday, and there was plenty of traffic, although the traffic noise petered off once we got to where we were going. When we got there, I felt the vehicle go up and down, like over a speed bump—or a threshold of some kind—and again, afterward, as we left the place, so I'm guessing we drove up and into a building, like some kind of garage or something."

"This guy, Doyle's abductor, did he give you his name?"

Father William lowered his head. "Yes, and I can give it to you," he said, "but only because Doyle told it to me *before* I heard his confession. He called him 'Alvaro.' But that's about all I can tell you."

"Thank you, Father," Vitelli said gently. "You've told us plenty. You've been a great help."

RIDING BACK INTO TOWN, Maddox said to Vitelli, "Sure would like to know everything that Gomez and Doyle told that priest in confession."

"Honestly, Eric," Vitelli answered, "I don't think it matters much. I'm pretty sure it would only tell us what we pretty well already know."

"Okay, then. We get back to my office we draw a circle around Stella Maris church. Figure that the driver could, at best, average thirty miles an hour driving around in the city at that time of day. Father figured they drove about a half hour, so we check out every warehouse and abandoned factory type building within a fifteen-mile radius of the church."

"Sounds good," Vitelli agreed.

Chapter 37

The FBI stakeout at the Western Avenue USPS Station was in its second day, and the evening team, four to midnight, was well into its shift at 10:05 PM.

The depot was a fairly new building: some yellow stone, metal, and glass. It looked more like a Walmart than a post office. The front of the building was all glass, with the service counter and the interior wall where the P.O. boxes were mounted, all in clear view from the street outside. Box 4385 was in the second tier of boxes, seven boxes over, and three boxes down, and the watchers had its position memorized.

"How long we gonna have to do this . . ." Special Agent Jim Crowley asked his partner, Special Agent Lars Dawson. ". . . stare at that stupid box?" The two men sat inside a Bureau-leased, black Chevrolet Suburban, parked on Western Avenue, just west of the front of the station.

"'Til the guy who looks like this sketch comes and opens up box 4385, I guess," Dawson replied. "Or until Maddox says we're done here."

"I hate this. Cops do stakeouts, not the FBI. And now I gotta pee."

"Use the bottle. That's what it's for, Crowley."

"I will not. That's just gross. There's a perfectly good public rest room inside that post office."

"You're kidding, right? Leave the stakeout to take a piss? Are you that fastidious?"

"I am what I am," Crowley replied, "and you can keep watch by yourself for the few minutes I'll be gone." And before Dawson could protest, Crowley was out of the car and into the post office.

Also keeping watch on the depot was Alexzander Popov, one of Korborov's lower-level henchman. He stood off in the shadows, and was under instruction to follow anyone who opened box 4385, which he could just see through the building's windowed exterior from where he stood. He knew there would be consequences if he messed up this assignment, and so he fought to stay alert. But it was rough: he had maintained his post for the past nine-or-so hours, coming here right after he got off his twelve-hour shift at the hospital.

ALVARO GOMEZ HAD LEFT Bobby Doyle in uneasy sleep in his cell, and decided it was time to go and pick up his last paycheck. He had bragged to Doyle that he really did not need it, but the fact was that he had been bleeding cash for the past several months, and could really use the money.

He parked his aged Toyota a block from the depot and walked the rest of the way. He arrived there at 10:08 PM, just as the skies opened up. Alvaro ducked quickly inside the building to escape the downpour, shook himself off, and went directly to box 4385.

Dawson, watching through the windshield of the "company" Chevy, was busy starting the vehicle and turning on the windshield wipers when the rain began. He caught Gomez in his peripheral vision, entering the depot, but was lulled into a false sense of security by the absence of the expected moustache and pony tail.

Now inside the building, Gomez, key in hand, was approaching box 4385, as Crowley was exiting the men's room and making his way back outside. He paused at the doorway, just long enough to block his partner's field of vision, and for Gomez to open the box, and take out the envelope inside.

Taking a deep breath, and gathering up gumption to brave the downpour, Crowley opened the depot door and ran to the Chevy, once again blocking off Dawson's field of vision. Gomez, oblivious to the rainstorm, was out of the building, and on his way back to his car, by the time the drenched Crowley settled back into the passenger's seat alongside his partner.

"Well, Crowley, was a comfortable pee worth getting soaked for?" Dawson asked sarcastically.

"Shut the hell up," was the disgruntled reply.

But if the FBI stakeout team had missed the incursion into box 4385, a now very wet Alexzander Popov had not. The rain was letting up as he started up his motorbike, and then slowly followed Gomez back to his car. Popov stopped his bike long enough for Gomez to get into the Toyota, start it, and pull out into traffic. Then he followed him all the way back to the warehouse where Bobby Doyle was being held prisoner.

Chapter 38

Earlier that same Tuesday, Maddox took Vitelli back at FBI headquarters, 1402 Twelfth Street, just east of Rush Avenue. Maddox quickly put a team to work doing just what both he and Vitelli had discussed in the car after their interview with Father William: identifying every warehouse and abandoned factory-type building with a fifteen-mile radius of Stella Maris church. Using blowups of Google maps made the job much easier, and, once again, Vitelli was blown away at the resources the feds could bring to bear that would never be available to Metro PD.

I would imagine Johnny Fowler knows all about Google maps and how to use them, but he would have been at it all by himself — I would be totally useless — working on nothing but his computer screen. It would have taken him all day to do what these guys did in a matter of hours, Vitelli mused.

"We've narrowed it down to about twenty-four possibilities, more or less — building that might or might not be the one we're looking for," Maddox said. "But it's getting late in the day. I'll have to get my guys on it first thing in the morning."

"We've got a few hours of daylight, left," Vitelli said. "Why not get right on it?"

"Because it will still take us the rest of the day to get the teams organized, parcel out the building assignments, get the vehicles, and set up, even to get them on the road first thing in the morning. That's why. And there's no guarantee we'll even be able to find what we're looking for, anyway!" Maddox countered.

"Okay, okay," Vitelli said.

"Look, Rich, I want to find Doyle as much as you do. But honestly, we're looking for that proverbial needle in the haystack. Anyway, I've already got teams out watching Gomez's P.O. box 'round the clock. I know we've got access to more manpower and assets than you guys do at Metro, but even *we* can only do so much."

"I understand," a chastened Vitelli replied. "First thing in the morning, then."

"Right," Maddox said.

Chapter 39

Alexzander Popov spoke into a burner phone. "I followed him to what looks like a warehouse building on Culver Avenue, just west of Fifty-Third Street. He was driving an old Toyota sedan, and he drove it right into the building. There's this big roll-up door in the front."

"Address? You got an address for this place?" Vasyli asked at the other end of the line.

"What address?" Popov replied. "No numbers on any of these buildings." This one is the fifth building on Culver, going west off Fifty-Third."

"Okay, Alexzander, you have done well. Viktor will be pleased. Stay there and we will be there shortly. Call me at this number if anything changes before we get there."

"I will," Popov replied, thrilled with the idea that Viktor Korborov might now know of his existence.

JUST BEFORE MIDNIGHT TUESDAY, arriving in a variety of vehicles: two SUVs; a van; and a pickup truck; were Viktor Korborov, his sidekick Vasyli, and five heavily-armed goons. They arrived at Culver Avenue, in front of the fifth building west of 53rd Street. A faithful Alexzander Popov greeted them with a broad smile. "He's still in there," he said. "The man who opened the post office box is still in there."

"Good," Vasyli said. "You have done good, Alexzander. You can take your bike and go now. We will take it from here."

An unhappy Popov left the scene as ordered, not looking forward to the immediately upcoming start of his twelve-hour shift at the hospital.

Vasyli busily determined the best way to breach the building with a minimum of noise; it was important, after all, to not advertise their presence to anyone who might be waiting inside. *No telling what artillery they might have available inside!* he thought.

Chapter 40

Vasyli need not have worried. There was nobody inside to greet them other than an unarmed Alvaro Gomez, who had been busily brushing his teeth and preparing for bed.

Vasyli's man had efficiently jimmied open the warehouse's access door, which was located next to the roll-up door in the front of the building. The Russians made minimal noise, and entered the building warily and stealthily. Gomez was taken completely by surprise, dressed only in his underwear. Overwhelmed and outmaneuvered, he was smart enough to offer no resistance. Just one of Vasyli's men was sufficient to march him out of the warehouse office, onto the empty main warehouse floor, there to meet Viktor Korborov, who had just entered the building.

"If you wish to live through the night," Korborov said, "take us to Bobby Doyle."

A now thoroughly terrified Alvaro Gomez reluctantly led the Russians to the building-within-a-building, and the cage holding Bobby Doyle. The room's miasma didn't appear to faze Korborov or his men in the least. Doyle, thinking that the police had come to rescue him, greeted Korborov and his thugs with "Boy, am I glad to see you guys!"

Korborov's sneering "Are you now?" reply took Doyle aback, as it quickly dawned on the poor prisoner that his troubles had just suddenly increased, not decreased.

"Who are *you*?" Doyle pleaded, but was totally ignored.

"Key?" Korborov asked Gomez, pointing to the padlock on the cage door.

"The office. Desk drawer," Gomez replied. "Same key ring as my car keys." Vasyli didn't have to be told; he immediately left and returned a minute later with Gomez's keys.

"Found this with them," he said to Korborov, producing a hand gun: a Ruger .22-caliber target pistol.

"Yours?" Korborov addressed Gomez, and when he nodded, Korborov laughed aloud. "And who did you expect to hurt with that little popgun?"

Chastened and sullen, Gomez said nothing in reply. Korborov nodded to Vasyli, who hit Gomez hard across the face with the pistol. "Speak when spoken to!" Vasyli shouted.

"Doyle!" Alvaro answered, blood now running from his nose and a red gash across his face. "I was gonna use it to kill Bobby Doyle!"

Korborov chuckled. "Well," he said, "I suppose if you got close enough, and picked just the right spot, it *might* kill him. I would use something much bigger, of course, but I am not the expert marksman you must be! And why, exactly, were you planning to kill Bobby Doyle?"

But when Alvaro started to answer, Korborov stopped him. "Never mind. Time enough for that later." Then he turned to Vasyli. "Take them," he said, "and load them into the van. We must assume the *politsiya* will soon find this place as easily as we did."

Chapter 41

It had bothered Vitelli all that afternoon and all the way on his drive home that same Tuesday evening: *I could swear that nun, the one in white, was Leona! If not, she sure as blazes was a dead ringer for her. 'Sister Lucy Simic.' I know that name, too — Lucy Simic. I'm sure of it — one of her aliases. But it* can't *be her!*

The Leona I knew has to be halfway across the world, holed up somewhere. She got out of the country with millions, could go anywhere she wanted, so why, in the name of all that is reasonable, would she come back here, to this city, of all places? And hide out as a nun? Who does that? So, no, the novice nun in the white habit can't *be her! Just can't be.*

By the time he arrived home, and parked his Rogue in his spot, Vitelli had pretty much convinced himself that it had been a simple case of mistaken identity. The nun in white was just a Leona lookalike — had to be. But, in the back of his mind, the name, Lucy Simic, was just too much of a coincidence; and he knew there were was no such thing as a coincidence.

Inside his place, Vitelli grabbed a bottle of Semple beer from the fridge, took a healthy swig, and then fed the cats. He then fried up a patty of ground beef for a hamburger, while some packaged frozen French fries baked in the toaster oven. The burger was done, but the fries weren't, so he threw together a salad using some romaine that had been in the fridge for at least a week, and an equally ancient tomato. He dressed it with a bottled ranch salad dressing that he had opened and refrigerated at least a month earlier. With the beef patty now lodged between two slices of whole wheat bread, Vitelli sat down to what he considered was a home-cooked meal.

He remembered to clean out the cats' litter box before he turned into bed for the night, after watching a hockey game on TV: The Rangers vs. the Lightning. The Lightning won with a last-minute goal, 2-1. He liked the Rangers, and was disappointed with the loss, but consoled himself with the thought that the season was still young.

That night, for whatever reason, he dreamed about Pam, the attractive woman he had briefly met at church. In the dream, she cooked him a hamburger, and told him he needed to get out more. The two of them were in one of those dance clubs with all the strobe lights, trying to slow dance to some techno music, when Leona broke in, pushed Pam away, and started dancing with him. And then the alarm went off. He luxuriated in bed for just a few minutes, Tristan and Isolde rubbing against him, purring for their breakfast.

When this Bobby Doyle case is over, he thought, *I'll go back to that school and make sure I was mistaken about that nun.* Then it occurred to him: *What if she really is Leona, and she saw me, too, and has already skipped town?*

Then Vitelli consoled himself with the thought that if that were so, then it was too late to do anything about it anyway.

Chapter 42

When they got back to the mob headquarters that same night, actually in the wee hours on Wednesday, Korborov's henchmen escorted both Doyle and Gomez down to the basement. Noting the time, and even though he knew Anubis Cline kept strange hours, Korborov decided to wait until morning before calling Cline and informing him of the evening's successful endeavors. *Besides,* Korborov considered, *maybe Cline does not need his sleep, but I do!*

Before retiring to his rooms in the upper part of the building, Korborov instructed Vasyli to "Shackle Doyle to something solid so he cannot go anywhere. I will interrogate the other one in the morning, so soften him up a bit for me, eh?"

"My pleasure," Vasyli replied.

"The boy's gun. Where is it?"

"I have it," Vasyli said. "Do you want it?"

"I do. As a keepsake."

"I will send it up to you."

"*Khoroshiy.* Good. And if Sonya is already asleep, wake her and send her up to me. I need a little relaxation before sleeping, no?"

Vasyli grinned, and nodded in understanding.

THE TV METEOROLOGIST REPORTED on the Wednesday early morning news broadcast that a "bomb cyclone" was on its way to the city: a blast of Artic air that would bring with it unseasonable freezing temperatures, high winds, and possibly several inches of snow.

The weather news didn't faze Korborov in the least. This time of year, in Russia, the streets would already be unpassable and ice and snow would be everywhere. *These people don't know what bad weather is,* he mused, as he sat warm and comfortable, enjoying his usual breakfast of just bread and black tea.

When he had finished eating, Korborov went to the basement to "interview" Alvaro Gomez. He found Alvaro much as he had found Arnold Schuster, a battered body, naked and tied to a chair. Once again, Vasyli was in attendance, but this time, another person was in the audience: Bobby Doyle, who was shackled to a nearby building support column and could see and hear everything that went on. He had spent the night witnessing the "softening" of his erstwhile captor, and, other than from sheer exhaustion, had slept very little.

"Ah, Vasyli," Korborov said, addressing his man, "what did I tell you about wearing gloves when you are working? See, your hands are bleeding again."

"The scabs from last time broke, and my knuckles started bleeding again," Vasyli explained, grinning.

Korborov smiled back at the giant and turned his attention to Alvaro Gomez. "Ah, Mr. Gomez, I trust you enjoyed the warm welcome Vasyli, here, has provided, no?" he asked.

But Korborov could see (to his satisfaction) that his sense of humor was wasted on Gomez, who proffered no answer. Korborov nodded to Vasyli, who lifted his leg and smashed the heel of his boot into Gomez's genitals. Alvaro screamed in pain. Observing this, Doyle winced in sympathetic agony.

"You will speak to me when I ask you a question, no?" Korborov said in a gentle, even voice.

Just able to get the words out, Alvaro answered, "Yes."

"Much better. Shall we get to it then? My name is Viktor Korborov, and I am the person who will decide whether you live or die. Now I know you are still quite capable of speech, and I can assure you that as long as you tell me what I want to know, and tell me only the truth, that Vasyli here, will do you no further harm. Do you understand me?"

Alvaro nodded his understanding.

"No," Korborov said. "Shaking your head will not do." He raised his voice. "Do you need to have Vasyli here remind you to speak when I ask you a question?"

"Please, no!"

"So, you understand me?"

"Yes," Alvaro answered weakly, "I understand you."

"Good. Now you will start from the beginning, and you will tell me why you abducted Bobby Doyle, and why you were holding him captive."

And then Alvaro Gomez told Korborov the entire story of he and his family's grievance against Bobby Doyle, what he had resolved to do about it, and how he had gone about it.

When he had heard the entirety of Alvaro's tale, Korborov told Vasyli in Russian to give him some water. "And keep him alive for the time being. I might possibly have more need of him later. And give Doyle some water, too."

Then Korborov went back upstairs to call Anubis Cline, to give him the good news.

Chapter 43

Alvaro and Bobby Doyle now found themselves alone in the building's basement. Alvaro was still tied to the chair, Doyle still shackled to the column. Doyle spoke first.

"I'm so sorry, Al, nobody deserves to go through what you just went through."

"Yeah, well, I didn't feel a whole hell of a lot after the first hour or so. I'm guessing now that when they figure they don't need me anymore, that this Korborov bastard is going to have that big goon of his finish me off. Not that I don't deserve it, for being stupid enough not to have killed you right off. No idea how these goons found us, but it's gotta be my fault—this is all on me."

"Look, Al, for what it's worth, I'm also sorry for what I did to your sister. Anyway, there's a good chance that this Korborov prick will finish the job you started out to do."

"No, no chance of that. The Marauders will pay a bundle to get you back in one piece. You're a hell of a lot more valuable to these Russian sonsabitches alive than dead. Me, on the other hand . . ."

"Don't talk like that. Pray, man. You'll get through this somehow. We both will."

"Be nice," Alvaro said. "But I don't think so. I, at least, am dead meat."

"ANUBIS?" VIKTOR KORBOROV SPOKE into the phone on Cline's secure line.

"Viktor," Cline replied, "to what do I owe the honor?"

"I have some good news, Anubis. I have Bobby Doyle in custody. He is alive and well."

"Good, Viktor. The Marauders will be happy to get their star quarterback returned to the team."

"I am sure they will. The question is how much they are willing to pay for his return."

"What ever can you mean, Viktor? You know as well as I that the reward being offered for his return is fifty thousand dollars,"

Korborov laughed out loud into the phone. "Come now, Anubis, you know quite well that any given night I take that much off the street in a few hours! I was thinking more in terms of five *million* dollars." Korborov heard Cline grunt into the phone; it was what passed for *his* laugh.

"Come now, Viktor. Must I remind you that kidnapping is a capital crime? Even if the team was willing to consider paying a ransom for him, Doyle was drafted by the Marauders in the *eleventh* round. He came to the team making the league's starting salary, that's just six hundred and sixty thousand dollars *per annum*. Let's see, now, the season, assuming the Marauders make the playoffs, is about a third over. So, Doyle has just four hundred and thirty-five thousand left to pay out on his contract. Perhaps I can persuade the team to pay that much to get him back . . ."

"Stop toying with me!" Korborov shouted into the phone. "You will pay the five million, or I will kill him! What will he be worth to you then, eh?"

Cline spoke calmly into the phone. "In that case, Viktor, I can assure you that the favor you asked of me earlier will never happen. Your group will never get the stadium concessions contract."

"The concessions contract is not worth five million dollars either! I am telling you, you *mu-dak,* either come up with the money or your player is a dead man!"

Again, calmly, Cline replied, "Language, Viktor, language! Must I remind you again that kidnapping is a capital crime? But so also is murder! Return Doyle alive and unharmed and the fifty thousand reward money is yours. I might even be persuaded to consider paying another half million for him. Otherwise—"

Korborov slammed down the phone. In his fury, he grabbed Alvaro's pistol, and, intent on murder, headed for the elevator that would take him down to the basement.

Chapter 44

That same Wednesday morning, FBI fielded four, three-man teams. Each team was tasked with investigating a list of addresses: possible locations within fifteen miles of Stella Maris church; and places which might possibly be Bobby Doyle's prison. The weather that day had started off nicely, with hazy sunshine and the light breeze comfortably cool.

It was mid-morning, the wind was picking up, the sun was now hidden behind a blanket of thick clouds; the weather was beginning to turn much colder. It was then that one of the teams came to a warehouse building on Culver Avenue, just west of 53rd Street. They noted that the building's access door from the street had been vandalized and was partially open. That was excuse enough to justify entering the building. Inside, they found an old model, green Toyota Corolla. Built against the far wall of the building, away from the street, was some sort of wooden-framed, building-within-a-building. Inside that was a steel cage built of steel rebar, the door to the cage swung open wide. A stinking bucket in the corner of the cage lent the room a distinctly unpleasant odor. The team leader knew right away that they had found the place where Bobby Doyle had been held prisoner.

And that they had found it too late.

As soon as the team reported in, Maddox got on the line to Vitelli, and gave him the bad news. Then Vitelli gave the same bad news to Captain Parker.

Chapter 45

For as long as he could remember, Vasyli's life revolved around the mob. The mob, after all, provided the big man everything he needed: the occasional woman to scratch that particular intermittent itch, and a regular outlet for his need to inflict serious pain. He had a place of his own, a walk-up not too far from the mob headquarters, but he rarely went there. On nights such as this, when there were victims in play, he preferred to stay close to where the action was: close to Viktor Korborov. So, if there was a need for sleep, he slept on a cot in a room off the basement.

This room was right next to the elevator, and every time the elevator was used, the mechanism in the pit at the base of the elevator shaft would creak and grown. And every time the elevator mechanism spoke to him, even in deepest sleep, Vasyli awoke. He awoke because the elevator was being operated, and only Viktor used the elevator.

And so it was that Wednesday morning, the elevator was on its way down. Viktor was coming, and Vasyli arose immediately to see what his boss wanted. He was already outside the door to his room and the elevator had not yet arrived. Just before the elevator doors opened, Vasyli quickly surveyed the basement and saw that everything was as he had left it: the naked man called Gomez was still tied to the chair, head down in fitful sleep; the big black man was still chained to the support column, sitting at its base, legs splayed out in front of him, also asleep.

But both prisoners were jolted awake when the elevator doors finally opened, and a furious Viktor Korborov, shouting obscenities in Russian, strode purposely over to a wide-eyed Bobby Doyle, pointed the pistol in his hand at Doyle's forehead and fired. The .22-caliber bullet was small, but it was sufficient. Doyle was killed instantly, the startled look on his face frozen, unchanged even as his head slumped forward in death.

Alvaro's left eye was swollen almost shut from his beating, his right eye less so. But he could see well enough. When he realized what he had just witnessed, Alvaro once again lost control over his bladder, and added to the puddle already beneath his chair.

Vasyli was only puzzled. Korborov rarely lost his temper, and he wondered what it was that had penetrated his boss's usually cool veneer.

Killing Bobby Doyle seemed somehow to have an almost instantaneous calming effect on Korborov. He walked slowly to where Vasyli stood, and handed him the pistol. Alvaro could hear him give Vasyli instructions in Russian, in a now normal, even-toned voice, Vasyli nodding his understanding.

When Korborov had gone, and Vasyli went about following his boss's orders, Alvaro was sickened even further by what he witnessed next.

Chapter 46

The rest of that Wednesday passed uneventfully at Metro Police headquarters. The weather had, just as the TV meteorologist foretold, become miserable: overcast, very cold—just above freezing—with high winds. But, so far at least, no snow.

It was evident that the Russians—they could not prove it, of course, but both Vitelli and Maddox were sure it was the Russians—had gained the upper hand, and now there was nothing either the police or the FBI could do, but watch, and wait and see how the Russians would play out their hand.

"I'm thinking their next move is to contact the Marauders and demand a ransom," Maddox said over the phone to Vitelli that afternoon. "I've told our people manning the hot line to expect it."

"That would certainly be the reasonable thing to do," Vitelli answered, "but they are a crazy bunch, and there's no telling."

"That's true, but they also like money. There is every reason to believe that Doyle was still very much alive when they nabbed him from Gomez's little cage. It would not make much sense, after all, to make off with a corpse. If we were likely to find anyone dead at that warehouse, it would have been Gomez."

"Yeah, but they took him too. Don't you wonder why that was?" Vitelli asked.

"I do, but I can't figure out why. Even if they were worried about his being a witness, he could hardly be a witness to anything if he was dead. You got any ideas?"

"One. But it's a little far-fetched. I'm thinkin' it speaks to the kind of man Viktor Korborov might just be. Maybe the Russians were able to discover that it was Gomez that abducted Doyle, and then found Doyle, in turn, by getting a line on Gomez. But we know *why* Gomez did what he did, and I don't think Korborov did. I think he took Gomez just to get his back story."

"Could be. Maybe Korborov is just that curious. But, either way, Gomez is a dead man when Viktor finds out whatever it is he wants to know."

"Yeah, probably," Vitelli agreed, "vicious bastard that Korborov seems to be."

"You mean *is*," Maddox said.

Chapter 47

Vitelli almost didn't go. The weather was crappy to begin with, and it was windy and freezing outside. *But I've been out in much worse, and at least it isn't snowing.*

But it certainly hadn't been anything like a formal invitation, and the only reason he would even dream of going was the instant attraction he had felt for the widow Pam whatever-her-last-name-was. *You know,* he thought, *the attractive woman with the tall, cool-lookin' dude attached.*

But, despite his trepidation and the nasty weather, to O'Toole's that Wednesday evening he went. He went, and, once there, headed for the back room where St. Anselm's "Over-Thirty Singles Group" met for dinner.

Vitelli was stopped at the entrance by a large smiling woman who sat at a table. She had a stick-on label on her dress that said "Hi, I'm" in print, with "Maybelle" written in below it. She also had a roll of blue tickets and a cash box.

"Tickets are ten dollars," she said, "and that's for dinner. Drinks are extra. Pay at the bar."

"Sure," Vitelli said, and took two fives out of his wallet and handed them to Maybelle.

"Your first time here," she said, still smiling. "I can tell. You're nervous, but, relax, you'll like it."

Vitelli couldn't think of anything to say to that, and just smiled back as he took the proffered ticket. "Fill out a name tag," she said, shoving a blank one at him, along with a blue marker. "Helps you get acquainted."

"Right," he said. He wrote "Rich" on the tag, pulled off the backing, and stuck it to the lapel of his sport jacket.

As he went in and looked around the room, he felt immediately out of place. In sport jacket and tie, he was overdressed. Everyone else was dressed casually, with the men in polo shirts and such, with jeans, and even some in shorts, the women in equally sporty clothes.

"Don't you look nice!" a throaty voice behind him said. He turned, and there was the widow Pam, the tall, slim, man with greying temples from last Sunday attached. She was wearing a light blue, print, summer dress, well out of step with the worsening weather outside. "My fault," she said, smiling broadly. "I should have told you casual dress. But, never mind. Just lose the tie, and you'll be fine."

"Right," the man next to her said, studying Vitelli's name tag. "Rich, is it? Hi, I'm John Karns, Pam's brother."

"Right. John. Pam's brother. Pleased to meet you!" Now things were *definitely* looking up.

Of course, it had not exactly been a date, but almost. And he left that night still not knowing her last name.

Chapter 48

That frigid Thursday morning, Anubis Cline's housekeeper took receipt of a FedEx package sent to Cline's West Lakeside mansion at 11456 Lakeview Place. The package was fairly heavy, a corrugated carton cube, measuring about a foot in any dimension.

Cline was in his office, a room across from his former bedroom, loaded with computers, file cabinets, an office safe, a huge walnut-finished desk, and a brocade-covered settee under the window that looked out over Lakeview Place. Cline was sitting at his desk, at a computer, reading the reports from the European markets. He was dressed the same way he was hours earlier, when he got up to get the early market reports: still in the underwear he slept in, his bulk covered in a tentlike, white terry-cloth robe.

"This just came for you," the housekeeper said, setting the box on the empty corner of the desk.

"Thank you," Cline acknowledged, waving her off with his hand, as he studied his computer screen.

The box lay where it was put for another half hour before Cline thought to open it. When he did open it, the contents managed to disturb even the studied equanimity of Anubis Cline.

Staring up at Cline from the box were the sightless eyes in the severed head of Bobby Doyle.

"Good God!" was the only thing that the avowed atheist Cline could think to exclaim.

That same morning, after a night when the temperature had fallen below freezing, two more bodies were found in an empty lot. It was a lot not far from the one that had held the corpses of Arnold Schuster and Horace Blake, not a week earlier. One body, the build and bulk unmistakable, could only be the headless corpse of Bobby Doyle. The other was the naked body of an unidentified male, his head inside a plastic bag. Remarkably, however, the second body was still alive, if only barely so.

Chapter 49

By nine, Thursday morning, the report had already come into missing persons from homicide, concerning the two bodies found in another vacant lot out by the railyards, not far from where the corpses of Arnold Schuster and Horace Blake had been found the previous Saturday.

Using the corpse's fingerprints, the coroner confirmed that the one, headless, body, was that of Bobby Doyle. The second body, the unidentified male, was still hanging onto life, and was now in intensive care at Metro General. *How in blazes did the man survive?* Vitelli asked himself, *with a plastic bag over his head, and the weather below freezing? Well, at least it didn't snow and cover up the bodies, or they'd never have been found!*

Vitelli was pretty sure that the person in ICU was Alvaro Gomez, and immediately arranged for a uniformed officer to stand guard over this second person around the clock. But he needed a positive identification, and so he called Eric Maddox; he was not surprised to learn that he had already been apprised of the two bodies found in the empty lot.

"And you want a positive ID on the second person you figure is probably Alvaro Gomez. Me too, and I'm already on it," Maddox said. "I contacted the Boston office. They're getting hold of Violetta Gomez, first thing, to see if she has anything that might have Alvaro's DNA on it. If she does, they can run it and send us the profile."

"Good idea. But I'd hate to be the agent who would have to tell his mother that her son may well be lying in the hospital right now, in critical condition, and may not make it."

"Me neither."

Vitelli did a pass at Captain Parker's office on his way out to Metro General, bringing him up to speed. Parker took in the information stoically.

"Geez," Parker finally said, "the fact that one of them is still alive is something, at least. But, when whoever it was that wanted him dead in the first place, finds out they botched the job, they're only gonna wanna come back and finish it."

"True. And about that, we're gonna have to put out a media release at some point," Vitelli reminded Parker. "They already have gotten wind of the two bodies found, and my guess is that they will go ballistic when they find out that one of them was Bobby Doyle. And once they hear his head was missing . . . they'll go nuts. Can we just not tell them that the second man is still alive?"

"Yeah, well," Parker said, "that would be withholding information from the public, and it's not at all certain he's gonna stay that way, anyway, is it? I think I'll just pass that particular problem upstairs. Let the mayor and the commissioner deal with that decision, and with the media in general. Our job is to find the bastards responsible."

"Okay, then, I'm headed to Metro General to find out whatever I can."

"Good luck!"

AS VITELLI WAS ON his way to the hospital, Metro Homicide received a call from Anubis Cline, reporting the grisly package that he has just opened. Homicide dispatched Detective Sam Levinson to Cline's home; ironically, it was Levinson who also first responded to the report of the murder of Cline's ward, Jael, and the subsequent killing of Charlene Morton by Cline a year earlier.

Vitelli arrived at the hospital just as the uniformed officer arrived to guard the still-unidentified ICU patient. "You can't go in there," the ICU nurse said, when Vitelli arrived outside the room where the man he was sure was Gomez was being treated. The name tag on her blue-green scrubs read "Evelyn Krause, RN, BSN." Scrubs are not exactly designed to make a person look attractive, but nurse Krause was really quite pretty. She was a head shorter than Vitelli, strawberry blonde hair tied back in a bun, high cheekbones, pert nose, emerald eyes.

"Okay, then," Vitelli replied, "but I'm Metro Police." He showed her his ID, she inspected it, and said, "Okay, Lieutenant—Vitelli, is it?—but you still can't go in there."

"Well, if he is who I think he is, he's a wanted man, and I'm posting a uniformed officer outside his room twenty-four, seven."

"Fine," she said, "but he can't go in either. Besides, the patient is listed as critical, and won't be in any condition to go anywhere anytime soon. His blood oxygen level was dangerously low on arrival, and he was at risk for cerebral ischemia, so the doctor put him on a ventilator. All his vitals are steady for the time being, but he's being monitored continuously.

"So I assumed. Not all that medical part, maybe, but he figured to be in pretty bad shape. We figure somebody tried to murder him and failed. What I'm worried about is someone trying to come in and finish the job."

That got the nurse's attention. "I see," she said. "In that case, is there anything we can do to make your officer comfortable?"

"He'll be fine. Tell me, nurse Krause, what did your patient look like when he in when he was brought in here? Did the EMTs say what condition he was in when they found him?"

"I was here on duty when they brought him in. He was beaten up pretty bad, and was covered with blood. The EMTs who brought him in said he had had a plastic bag put over his head, but that when they removed it, they saw that he had somehow managed to make a hole in the bag at his mouth, and was evidently able to take in just enough air through it to stay alive. As I said, the doctor is worried that, what with probable oxygen deprivation, there could well be some brain damage. Hence the ventilator. It was also freezing outside overnight, and the patient was found naked, and unsurprisingly showed signs of hypothermia as well. Frankly, it's a miracle that he even survived the night."

"Wow," Vitelli said. Then he got another thought. "You said he'd been found all beaten up and bloody. I assume the hospital cleaned him up?"

"We did," the nurse replied, "or rather *I* did. That bio waste bin over there is loaded with all the wipes it took to clean him up."

"Great. But, nurse, that's now evidence. I need you to bag all those wipes and give them to me."

"You can just take the whole container with you," she said.

"Even better," Vitelli answered.

"But why? How are a bunch of bloody rags evidence?"

"Well, the rags have the victim's blood on them, and chances are, also the blood of the man who beat him up. That's DNA evidence. And I'm betting that the man who beat up your patient also beat two other men to death just last week. Besides, I need a DNA sample from your patient anyway to confirm that he is who I think he is."

"Never thought about any of that," she said. "But that makes sense. Two other men you say? Now I'm really glad you're putting a policeman up here."

"I need you to certify that the container you're giving me is holding the wipes you used to clean up the victim — can you do that?"

"I can."

"Good. Now when do you think I'll be able to interview the victim?"

"You'll have to ask the doctor that. Doctor Madison Fish is the neurologist in attendance. But my guess is that it will be at least a couple of days before that happens, if then."

"Doctor Fish, is it? Okay, I'll ask him. And thank you for your help."

Vitelli tracked down Dr. Fish, and found a gaunt, tall, man in the proverbial white coat with draped stethoscope. A narrow-faced man with black-rimmed glasses and steely gray eyes, Fish gave him exactly the same assessment as had nurse Krause. Vitelli resigned himself to the fact that *if* this indeed was Alvaro Gomez, it might be days, or even weeks, before he could be interviewed — assuming he could ever be interviewed at all.

Chapter 50

No sooner did Vitelli return to his office after dropping off the container of bloody wipes to the forensics lab, when Captain Parker grabbed him. "Get your ass down to Anubis Cline's place. Homicide says Cline got Bobby Doyle's missing head mailed to him in a box this morning."

"Holy shit," was all Vitelli could say as he made his way back out the door. In the car, on the way to Cline's mansion, he called Eric Maddox.

"I heard," was all Maddox said. "I'll meet you there."

MADDOX WAS WAITING AT Cline's when Vitelli arrived. He was outside the house, talking to Sam Levinson in the driveway.

When he first saw it, a year earlier, Vitelli thought that Cline's West Lakeside mansion was rather modest for a man of Cline's reputed wealth. But it was a tasteful building of fieldstone and redwood that sat on some of the most prime real estate in the city: high up on a bluff, with a magnificent view of the lake below.

"I've seen some weird shit," Levinson was saying as Vitelli approached, "but this beats all. Here's this face staring up at you, one you'd seen in the papers and on TV, dozens of times, all gray and ashen, dead eyes wide open and glazed over, with this bullet hole right in the middle of his forehead. Just beats all."

"Where's it now?" Maddox asked.

"Forensics took it," Levison said, "and they're damn well welcome to it."

"You interview Cline?" Vitelli asked.

"Not yet. Figured this was your case—originally, anyway. So I thought I'd wait and let you and Maddox here take the lead."

"Thanks," Vitelli and Maddox spoke practically in unison.

THE TRIO WAS LED by his housekeeper to Anubis Cline's home office, a room Vitelli remembered, which was just across the hallway from the bedroom where Cline's ward, Jael, had been murdered. On the way, Vitelli noted something he thought rather strange, if not downright maudlin. On the mantle above the huge stone fireplace was a gold urn with the letter "J" on it. On either side of the urn was a vase of freshly-cut flowers.

They found Anubis Cline sitting at the desk in his office, studying a computer screen. His huge form was now hidden beneath one of the white linen suits he affected. The phrase *"Face like a bag of rocks,"* flashed across Vitelli's mind's eye.

"Be with you gentlemen momentarily," Cline said, without looking up from his computer screen. He typed something into the computer with two fingers, then pushed back from his desk, and finally looked up at his visitors. "Now, how can I be of service?" he asked.

Maddox took the lead. "I'm FBI Special Agent Eric Maddox, and these gentlemen are Detectives Vitelli and Levenson." Vitelli and Levenson nodded as their names were mentioned.

"Yes," Cline acknowledged, "I remember all three of you gentlemen from the unfortunate events of a year or so ago. You will excuse me for saying so, but I would just as soon not to have renewed our acquaintance." He grimaced into what, for him, passed as a smile.

"I understand perfectly," Maddox said, "but unfortunate circumstances have made our reacquaintance necessary.

Now, tell me, what do you think brought about your receiving that package this morning?"

"Come now, Agent Maddox, let's not beat about the bush, shall we? You're obviously referring to my having received Bobby Doyle's severed head in a box this morning." He paused, as if to make his possibly feigned show of aplomb more convincing. "And, yes, I believe I can provide a plausible explanation for my having received it."

"Go on, Mr. Cline," Maddox said.

"Very well, then," Cline replied. "First, you must understand that it is widely known that I control the purse strings of the Marauders football organization. It was me, for example, who set the reward for any information leading to Bobby Doyle's recovery at fifty thousand dollars. I have been severely criticized both inside and outside the Marauders organization, I assure you, for offering what many of my colleagues in the consortium thought was far too little. But I assure you, gentlemen, I had my reasons."

Perhaps you did, Vitelli mused, *but maybe you're just a cheapskate playing with other people's lives.*

"It was Wednesday last, I believe," Cline continued, "when I received this telephone call. Now I can only assume the caller knew that I am the Marauders' money man, and called me direct for that reason, rather than go through the hot line. In any case, the caller tried to extort the sum of fifty million dollars for the return of Bobby Doyle."

"Did the caller identify himself in any way?" Maddox asked.

"He did not, and he had some sort of device on the line to disguise his voice," Cline lied. "Nor did he offer me any proof that he did indeed have Mr. Doyle in his possession. Nonetheless, I attempted to negotiate with him, offering a far lesser amount if he returned Mr. Doyle unharmed. The caller became very upset and began to shout obscenities over the phone, threating to kill or maim Bobby unless I assented to the five-million-dollar figure. When, again, I flatly refused, he hung up on me."

"And you think that your caller was the person who sent you this morning's package?" Maddox asked.

"I can only assume so," Cline replied.

"And you have no clue who this person might be?" Vitelli asked.

"Not really. But there was this one thing, the caller called me a '*mu-dak*.'"

"A *mu-dak*?" Maddox repeated.

"Yes, Agent Maddox. *Mu-dak* is the Russian equivalent of 'prick.'"

Chapter 51

The city's newly elected Mayor, a black woman who had served as the city council's official gadfly during the previous administration, had no choice but to call a press conference. Together with the police commissioner, she faced a boisterous and unruly crowd of reporters.

The very first question was asked by a reporter from Fox News: "Is it true, Madam Mayor, that the Marauders' owners received Bobby Doyle's head in the mail this morning?"

"It is," she replied. A collective groan arose from the assembled news people.

"And that Bobby Doyle was murdered only after the Marauders' owners refused to pay the kidnapper's ransom demands?" the Fox reporter continued.

"That appears to be idle speculation," the mayor parried.

And, for the mayor and police commissioner at least, the press conference went downhill from there.

Just minutes after the media circus had finally wrapped up, the Marauders organization issued an official statement over the signature of Frank Daugherty, the spokesman for the team owners:

> "The entire Marauders organization shares the public's grief over the senseless abduction and murder of Bobby Doyle. While Bobby can never be replaced, the rest of the team will soldier on through the rest of the season as best it can. The team will also do the best it can to cooperate with law enforcement to bring Bobby's murderers to justice. To that end, we are posting a $250,000 reward for any information leading to the arrest of the person or persons responsible for this heinous crime."

Chapter 52

Viktor Korborov was dressing down his man Vasyli, yelling at him in Russian.

"How could you be so stupid? The man was half dead when he left here — all you had to do was finish the job!"

"I am sorry, Boss. I did just as we always do. I tied the plastic bag around his head. I swear Gomez was not breathing when I left him in that lot next to Doyle."

"Well, he is apparently breathing well enough now! Our man Popov at Metro General says he is in intensive care and they are giving him fluids. They do not give fluids to a dead man!"

Vasyli said nothing. He had messed up and he knew it. "I do not understand it," Vasyli pleaded, "how he could he possibly still be alive. I tied the plastic bag firmly around his head. Besides, it was freezing out, and the man was stark naked!"

"The worst part," Korborov continued his rant, "is that Gomez saw me shoot Doyle. A live witness! Did you at least get rid of the gun?"

"I did, Boss. I wiped it clean and threw it in a dumpster at least six blocks away from where I dumped the bodies."

Korborov, Vasyli, noted, at least had stopped yelling. "Then there was that, at least. Probably off in the landfill by now," Korborov said, finally back to his normal voice.

"Let me make it right, Boss. I will go myself to the hospital and finish Gomez."

"Do not be stupid. You are far too big to get anywhere near him unnoticed. Besides, our man there says they have a continuous police guard on him, and anyone in intensive care is closely monitored all the time anyway."

"Can our man get to him?"

"Eventually perhaps, assuming he has the stomach for it. But right now, it would be impossible. We will just have to wait and see. As you said, Gomez was practically dead when he left here anyway. With any luck, he will just go ahead and finish dying."

But luck was not with Korborov that day. At Metro General, though still classified as "in critical condition," Alvaro Gomez continued to cling to life.

Chapter 53

Friday morning found Anubis Cline still in his home office when Viktor Korborov made a call from a burner phone to Cline's secure land line.

"So, Anubis, you received my little gift?"

"I did." Cline did his best to sound somber.

"So, I would count us as even for now."

"How so, Viktor?"

"I collected no reward," Korborov replied, amusement dripping from his voice, "but your American football team has no star player. Your golden boy is gone forever, and there will be no chance now for the big championship and a big payday for the team! From where I sit, it would seem that you have caught what you people call 'the short end of the stick,' no?"

"If you say so, Viktor. So it *would* appear."

But Korborov never caught the subtleness in Cline's reply. "Until next time, then, eh?" Korborov said, and hung up the phone.

THAT SAME FRIDAY AFTERNOON at One Marauder Place, the group of six men and three women who made up the consortium that owned the team, gathered at the long laminate table in the tower conference room. All were dressed in what might be considered "sports casual." All of the men were past fifty, some well past, all with at least some grey in whatever hair remained. The three women were all older—over sixty—and had fought their way bitterly to the top in their professional life. Each woman had blasted her way through the proverbial "glass ceiling" some decades earlier, and had never looked back.

Of course, it was Anubis Cline who conducted the meeting.

The eight other people who had bought into the consortium had done so for various reasons, and most of them had originally contributed far more to buy the franchise than had Cline. Yet it was Cline who ran the club, controlled the money, and called all the shots. That was because all five of the other men and the three women were all, in some way or other, beholden to Cline. He had, in short, enough dirt on each one of them, so that they did just as they were told — not that it had been all that bad an experience.

Cline had run the team with the financial ledgers open to each of them, and he had, to date, run it very well. There were, of course, some steep losses in the beginning, and they all — Cline included — suffered through those first days in direct proportion to their original investments.

But now the franchise had become insanely profitable, and, again, in direct proportion to their investments, they had shared in those profits. They were loath to admit it, but the loathsome Cline had done quite well by each of them.

Now the group had been assembled to discuss the way forward after the events of the past several days. The assembled mood (save for, strangely enough, Cline's) was, needless to say, grim.

"Well, ladies and gentlemen," Cline began, "we seem to have lost our star player." There was a collective groan from the others. "But I am here to assure you that all is not lost."

Cline scanned the room, with its walnut-paneled interior wall and three glass outer walls overlooking downtown, and did his best to look assuring. But conveying emotion of any kind to others was not his strong suit. He continued: "I want you all to know that prior to Bobby Doyle's unfortunate demise, I was contacted by his kidnappers, who demanded a five-million-dollar ransom for his return. I refused to pay it."

The eight others looked at each other in surprise. Dorothy Farber, who had become the de-facto spokesperson for the others, spoke up, "Why on earth would you do that, Anubis?"

"Because, dear Dorothy, it would not have been in the financial interests of the club to have given in to the demand."

Farber scowled back. "Please explain," she said.

"Gladly," Cline continued. "First, let me ask when any of you last examined our financials?"

Farber looked around at the others; most shook their heads. "I haven't for several weeks, Anubis, and apparently neither have any of the rest of us." She smiled. "We have come to trust that you are more than capable of acting in the club's best interests, you see." Several of the others nodded slightly in agreement, but Cline could see, written on their faces, that they still questioned his refusal to pay the ransom.

"Thank you for that confidence, Dorothy," Cline said. "But surely you will have noted that the club routinely takes out death and dismemberment insurance on each of our star players. And that, at the beginning of the season, there had been no such policy on Bobby Doyle."

"No," Farber said, "but we did take out such a policy on Doyle once he became our starting quarterback. It was for five million dollars, I believe. I remembering questioning the amount, since he was only being paid the league starting salary. But you said he would soon be negotiating for more, and was worth at least that much. And I agreed that you were right."

"Yes," Cline acknowledged, "but five weeks ago I upped the coverage to fifty million." There were astounded looks all around. "It took another week for the insurance companies to cover such a sum among themselves, but eventually they formed a large enough consortium. And for a substantial monthly premium I might note. So you see, ladies and gentlemen, Bobby Doyle was worth much more to us dead than alive."

Dorothy Farber grinned. "Oh, Anubis!" she said, "that *is* harsh!"

Chapter 54

At Metro General, still in intensive care, the man thought to be Alvaro Gomez was still fighting for his life. One positive sign: the patient had been taken off the ventilator and was now breathing on his own.

Dr. Madison Fish, the neurologist who had been treating him, came in to run some tests. The worry was that even with the hole Gomez had somehow managed to poke in the plastic bag over his head, he still had not managed to breathe in enough oxygen to avoid brain damage.

"His body responses appear normal," Fish said to the attending ICU physician, "and his encephalogram would indicate normal brain function, considering his overall condition and sedation. But there is no way to say for sure whether there is brain damage or not until the patient is fully conscious."

"I would be very surprised if there is no brain damage," said the ICU doctor." And it's a wonder he didn't freeze to death, anyway, considering he spent the night naked, completely exposed to the freezing air."

"That might actually have been a good thing," Fish said. "The cold would have slowed his metabolism way down, and reduced his body's need for oxygen."

"You mean like the kid who fell through the ice in the lake last winter. He actually drowned, and was without air for at least fifteen minutes. The ice-cold water caused hypothermia, and when they pulled him out and brought his respiration back, he was none the worse for wear."

"Just so. There is every hope that a similar mechanism could be in play here. The human body is truly an amazing machine, after all," Fish said.

"It is that," the ICU doctor agreed.

Chapter 55

That Friday evening, Anubis Cline sat in his white terrycloth bathrobe sipping a twenty-one-year-old, single-malt Glenfiddich and smoking a Cuban cigar. He spoke in his mind to his dearly departed ward. He sat in front of the fireplace, directly underneath the solid gold urn that held his ward's ashes.

Well, Jael, my dear, my associates appeared to be somewhat pleasantly surprised when they learned that the tragedy of Bobby Doyle's demise was not so much of a tragedy after all!

"They should have known, Abba," his muse replied, "that you had the situation well in hand, as usual."

They certainly should have. Of course, they did not know that I, as a member of the Marauders' consortium, have an insurable interest in each of the club's star players in my own right, and that I personally had taken out a million-dollar death and dismemberment policy on Mister Doyle. In addition to our share in the larger policy, we will soon have an additional cool million dollars in our pocket.

"But how, Abba, could you be sure that Bobby Doyle would be kidnapped in the first place, let alone killed when a ransom was not forthcoming?"

Well, my dear, of course there was no way I could foresee Alvaro Gomez's vendetta against Doyle. Had I even known about it, I would certainly have questioned his ability to pull off actually abducting and imprisoning him. Nor could I have assumed that he might actually go through with killing Doyle. Hence my recruiting Korborov and his minions to find him before the authorities did.

"So clever, Abba! And if Mr. Gomez had not kidnapped Doyle?"

Then, Jael, my sweet, I had only to put a bug in Korborov's ear that kidnapping and ransoming Bobby Doyle might be a very lucrative exercise!

"Ah! But what if Korborov had accepted your offer of a lesser ransom, and not killed Doyle after all?"

Then, my dear, no harm, no foul. With the lesser ransom paid, the Marauders would have our star quarterback returned, and finish up what would have most likely been a very profitable season. As it stands, with the fan loyalty Doyle's demise will most likely generate, I expect the season will still be every bit as profitable.

"But with less chance of making the playoffs, and, possibly, even the league championship game."

True. But there was never any guarantee of that, now, was there?

"No, Abba, I suppose not. But the insurance money on the other hand . . ."

Exactly, my dear, exactly.

Chapter 56

Saturday came and went. The bomb cyclone from the Artic had come and gone, and it was, once again, still Autumn in the city—sunny and cold, but not unpleasantly so. Other cities to the north had not, however been so lightly touched by the weather. Minneapolis, for example, was still digging out from under forty-two inches of wet snow.

Vitelli started out his day with another brisk run, and was congratulating himself on his progress. *Not bad for an old man! Five miles in just under forty-five minutes. No record perhaps, but for me, that's my best time ever. Doubt I could have even done that in my twenties!*

He rewarded himself a hearty breakfast: two eggs, two sausage patties, a plain bagel, toasted, juice, and black coffee. *You got a precision machine, you got to fuel it!* he told himself.

He spent much of the day reading. He had bought himself a paperwhite Kindle, and had become addicted to e-books. There were plenty out there that were reasonably priced—at a fraction of the cost of a paperback—and he had even found a way to download some of the classics from the public library for free.

Out of a sense of duty perhaps, he thought to call Metro General later that afternoon and check on the condition of the man thought to be Gomez. Still alive, still no change. *It will be a miracle if he pulls through,* Vitelli pondered.

SOMEONE ELSE WAS ALSO interested in that man's condition, someone who knew for sure that the man in ICU was Alvaro Gomez. Viktor Korborov was still receiving regular reports from his man Alexzander Popov at Metro General. When his man continued to report that Gomez was still alive, but unresponsive, Korborov's thought: *Why do you not simplify my life, you miserable bastard? Just hurry up and die!*

Chapter 57

On Sunday morning, during the time Vitelli was at the ten o'clock Mass at St. Anselm's, the Metro General ICU patient thought to be Alvaro Gomez began to show some signs of approaching consciousness. Since being hooked up to a monitor on his arrival at Metro General, his vital signs had been typical for a patient in a comatose state; now his diastolic blood pressure had gone down to a more normal level, and his blood oxygen level was back above ninety percent.

The Metro Police forensics staff had run the bloody rags Vitelli had brought in from the hospital for DNA, and, indeed, one of the profiles was identical to that found on both bodies recovered eight days earlier. That was definite proof that the same person who had probably murdered both Arnold Schuster and Horace Blake, had also beaten up the man now fighting for his life at Metro General.

After Mass, Vitelli looked around in hope of seeing Pam Whatever-her-last-name-was, but she was nowhere to be seen. Disappointed, he went home and made brunch for himself.

THAT AFTERNOON AT FOUR, the Marauders were playing Carolina at home. Since the stadium had sold out, the league rules allowed the game to be broadcast on local TV. Vitelli was curious to see if Coach Ferguson would start the rookie Joe Coulter, or the veteran Sam McArdle. He settled in front of the TV at three-thirty with some snacks and some cold Semple's. The host of the pre-game show was positive Ferguson would start Coulter, but most of the discussion on the show centered around the tragic events of the week, and the grisly murder of Bobby Doyle.

When the Marauders took the field, each player wore a "BD 7" on his jersey: Doyle's initials and jersey number.

Carolina won the toss and elected to play defense; the Marauders would defend the south goal. When the Marauders' offense took the field for the first snap of the ball, it was McArdle who was behind center.

No telling what Ferguson had told the team that fired them up so, but the hapless Carolina team never stood a chance. The Marauders were up four scores at the half, with Carolina scoreless; only when the game was totally on ice, toward the end of the third quarter, did Coulter see any playing time. The final score was 42-6.

THAT SUNDAY EVENING AN off-duty patrolman ran across a homeless man attempting to sell a .22-caliber target pistol to a teenaged gangbanger. He flashed his shield and confiscated the weapon, which the homeless man said he had found while dumpster diving. Pocketing the pistol, the patrolman sent the others off with a warning. He never took their names and ended up keeping the pistol for himself.

Over that same weekend, two agents from the Boston FBI field office visited Violetta Gomez, now living in her daughter Juana Vargas' apartment. As gently as they could, they told her that an unconscious man in the hospital ICU, back in the city, could well be her son, Alvaro. Violetta went into hysterics, and her daughter Juana started screaming at them, shouting obscenities.

When things calmed down, they left the Vargas' apartment with an old hairbrush that had supposedly belonged to Alvaro Gomez.

The agents turned the hairbrush over to their lab with instructions to perform an expedited DNA analysis from human hair combed off the brush. Once the profile was obtained, it would immediately be sent electronically to Maddox's office back in the city.

Chapter 58

Monday morning found Vitelli in Captain Parker's office. "Anything from the feds on that DNA analysis coming in from Boston?" Parker asked.

"Nothing yet. But Eric Maddox promised to send it over as soon as he gets something."

"But you said you were pretty sure the guy in the hospital is our man Gomez."

"I did, and I still am. Everything fits. Height, weight, body type, even the pierced left earlobe. I'd be really surprised if it wasn't him."

"Yeah, but even if it is him, and he does somehow manage to wake up, who is to say he won't be a vegetable? No telling how long he went without air, and the poor bastard froze all night besides."

"Yeah, there is that. And even if he is our man, and does come to in a lucid state," Vitelli said, "he still may not be able to tell us much. We may never know who shot and killed Bobby Doyle. All he may be able to confirm is that the Russians were involved."

"That would be something, anyway. Geez, cutting off Doyle's head like that. At least the medical examiner said it was done post mortem. The ME said he couldn't even come up with a firm time of death for Doyle because the body was out in the cold so long. Best he could come up with is that Doyle was shot and killed with a .22-caliber firearm sometime last Wednesday morning. Says the weapon was fired at close range, and the bullet entered just above the bridge of Doyle's nose. Had to dig the .22-calbre slug out of the man's brain."

"Using a small-caliber weapon like that sounds more like the Italian mob than the Russians. But that may have been intentional — a ploy Korborov might have ordered to throw us off the scent."

"That damned Korborov!" Parker exclaimed. "How I'd love to get something on that bastard. We know he's responsible for half of the shit going down in this city. We've just never been able to prove any of it."

"That's because he never does any of the actual wet work himself, and the people who actually do it will never admit that Korborov's the one who ordered it. He runs his crew with an iron hand, and they would rather take a bullet for him than piss him off. And any witness out of the general public, anyone who may not be too frightened to speak up, ends up dead — like Arnold Schuster and Horace Blake."

Parker had no answer for that, just shook his head in agreement.

LATER THAT MONDAY, ERIC Maddox sent over the DNA profile from their lab in Boston. "Used some hair off a hairbrush the mother said was his," Maddox explained. Even a layman like Vitelli could see the markers were identical to one of the DNA profiles pulled off the bloody rags he retrieved from Metro General.

There was no question now. The man in the Metro General ICU ward was definitely Alvaro Gomez. At that moment a chilling thought passed through Vitelli's mind: *Now we're* sure *the comatose victim is Gomez. But that bastard Korborov knew that for sure all along! And, if I were Korborov, what plans would I already have in the works if Alvaro Gomez ever wakes up?*

Chapter 59

That same Monday, at Metro General, Alexzander Popov took note of the suddenly increased police presence outside Alvaro Gomez's ICU room. There were now two uniformed policemen on duty, along with a couple of men in suits—men whom he assumed were plainclothes Metro Police, but who were actually FBI agents. He knew something must have happened, but did not know what; as far as he could see, Gomez's condition had not changed.

In the wee hours of Tuesday morning, the alarms suddenly sounded simultaneously on the monitoring devices hooked up to Alvaro Gomez. The patient was quickly surrounded by ICU attendants and the on-duty doctor. The officers stationed outside knew something important had just happened, but they did not know what.

After his two-and-a-half days off, Alexzander Popov's schedule of twelve-hour shifts had just shifted; instead of the midnight-to-noon, graveyard shift, he was working days, from noon to midnight. So, he had not witnessed the Tuesday morning events in the ICU.

BOTH VITELLI AND ERIC Maddox got telephone calls at home Tuesday morning; Vitelli received his at 4:07 AM, Maddox just a few minutes later. Vitelli quickly got out of bed, got dressed, put some dry cat food out for Tristan and Isolde, and went out to brave the chill night air. Within the hour, both Vitelli and Maddox were on their way to Metro General.

Alvaro Gomez was awake, and was taking nourishment by mouth.

AT THAT HOUR OF the morning, there was no traffic, and Vitelli, blinking portable blue flasher attached to the Rogue's roof, blasted through the city. He arrived at Metro General in just under twenty minutes. Maddox lived farther out, and arrived some ten minutes later. But both men might just as well have stayed home. They could see from outside the room that Gomez was awake, sitting up, and apparently responding to the people around him. But the doctor in attendance was adamant. Under no circumstances would anyone but the medical team be allowed near him for the time being.

"And how long before we can talk to him?" Maddox and Vitelli asked the ICU doctor.

"No telling," the doctor replied. "He is awake, and he's able to talk some, and on the surface at least, Mr. Gomez appears to have not suffered any brain damage—or not very much, anyway. But it is probably too soon to tell without doing some tests. The neurologist, Doctor Fish, will be in later today to examine him, so we should know more later. In any case, it does not appear that he'll have to stay in the ICU much longer. But it will still be another day, at least, before he can be transferred to a regular room. Of course, it will be up to Doctor Fish, but my guess is that you will be able to talk to him then."

Vitelli and Maddox retired to the hospital cafeteria for breakfast. Maddox chose bacon, scrambled eggs, toast, and coffee. The bacon and toast both proved soggy; his eggs were rather dry and elderly. His coffee was thick and strong. He picked at his food and watched as Vitelli wolfed down an order of biscuits and sausage gravy.

"How can you eat that stuff?" Maddox asked.

Vitelli looked up in surprise. "Why?" he said, looking surprised. "Southern cooking. I love this stuff."

"If you say so," Maddox allowed, "but don't bother with the coffee. It's terrible."

Vitelli took a sip of his hitherto untouched cup. "It's not great," he said, "but it's pretty close to what I got used to in the Navy. Aboard ship, especially on the midnight watch, you were thankful if it was hot, and strong enough to keep you awake."

"Then I'm glad I did my stint in the Air Force," Maddox said.

Vitelli grinned. "Cake eaters," he said dismissively, and resumed his attack on the biscuits and gravy.

Maddox scowled, but made no comeback. They had rehearsed this gambit before. The Air Force, as the junior service, was always taking flak from the Army and the Navy. Instead, he asked, "So, what do you think? Should we wait around and see what happens with Gomez or head out to our respective offices?"

"Don't see what good waiting around to talk to Gomez would do. You heard what the doctor said. We don't get to talk to Gomez anytime soon. But that doesn't mean we shouldn't stick around for a while, and make some arrangements."

"What do you mean?" Maddox asked.

"I mean that someone tried very hard to kill Alvaro Gomez, and they were probably pretty sure that he was dead meat when they dropped him off in that empty lot. I'm thinking that if it's who we think it was, that the Russians have been watching Gomez just as intently as we have. And now that Gomez is awake, they will definitely pull out all the stops, and do their very damnedest to finish the job they started."

"Sounds about right. But what can they do? We already have four men guarding him around the clock."

"They could damn well put together an assault team, guys in balaclavas, wielding military hardware, and attack this place in force. These people wouldn't care how many

177

people they would have to take out along the way, either, just as long as they take out Gomez."

Maddox shuddered. "Damn, Vitelli, you're right. I wouldn't put it past Korborov to do just that."

"Okay, then," Vitelli said, and outlined a plan of action to Maddox that he had been thinking about for some time.

"Do you think that the hospital administration would cooperate?" he asked Maddox afterward.

"They will if both the Metro Police Department and the FBI tell them to," Maddox replied.

WHEN ALEXZANDER POPOV REPORTED in to work at noon on that same Tuesday, he was astonished to discover that Alvaro Gomez, although still in ICU, was awake, sitting up, and taking nourishment by mouth. Within minutes, he was on a burner phone to Viktor Korborov apprising him of this new turn of events.

Chapter 60

By Tuesday evening, Alvaro Gomez was stable enough to be moved to a regular hospital bed.

Metro General Hospital records would show, and anyone who enquired would be informed, that patient Alvaro Gomez had been transferred to room 418.

Room 418 was on the fourth floor of the west wing of the hospital, and the entire hospital staff knew that the west wing was currently not in use; it had been emptied out so that it could be completely remodeled as the hospital's new psychiatric wing. There were no patients in that wing, and all the old equipment had been removed. But under orders from the police and the FBI, the hospital staff had to return everything that had been removed from room 418 — bed and bedding, monitoring equipment, towels, toilet paper — everything.

As there had been at the ICU, four guards were also stationed outside room 418. But now they were wearing flak jackets and carrying military issue M4 rifles.

Among the hospital staff that had prepared the room for its new patient was an orderly named Alexzander Popov.

"IF EVERYBODY KNOWS GOMEZ is in that empty wing by himself, and the Russians come in force, then at least the collateral damage will be limited," Vitelli had reasoned, and Maddox agreed.

"But if they do come in force, no telling how many people Korborov will send. The man is not known for his subtle use of force," Maddox said.

"That's for sure, but I doubt Korborov will send more men than will look conspicuous in a hospital setting. I also seriously doubt he'd even attempt an all-out assault, shooting up the place floor-by-floor as he closes in on room 418. And even if he does send a crew he deems entirely expendable, I doubt they'll expose their weapons until they get to the fourth floor, west wing. No, I suspect he will try to be at least as subtle as that. But, whatever happens, let's just make sure we have a SWAT team on alert. Maybe we can't station an entire army on that floor, but at least the four guards that are there might be able to hold down the fort until SWAT arrives. Besides, Gomez won't be in 418 anyway."

"Right. He'll be down on the second floor, room 282, at the opposite end of the hospital. He should be well away from any potential action—or so we hope."

"Exactly," Vitelli agreed, "and maybe Korborov won't come after Gomez in the hospital anyway."

"I would," Maddox said.

VIKTOR KORBOROV WAS INFORMED of the arrangements made for Alvaro Gomez at Metro General just as soon as Alexzander Popov was able to get to a burner phone.

"Too late to move tonight," Korborov told Vasyli in Russian after he had hung up on the call from Popov. "We go tomorrow night, and this is what we will do . . ."

Chapter 61

Wednesday morning, ensconced in room 282, Alvaro Gomez was able to sit up and hold a conversation with Dr. Madison Fish. The neurologist spent some time examining him, probing, prodding, asking questions, reviewing test results.

"Well, Mister Gomez," he finally said, gazing down at him over the black-rimmed glasses that had slipped down on his long nose, "I don't know how you did it, but you appear to have made a full recovery."

Gomez grinned. "Thanks, Doc," he replied, "but the people here have been taking great care of me."

"I know they have," Fish agreed, "but no amount of care explains how you've managed to overcome what you have. Mister Gomez, when I first examined you, you were at death's door. I am truly amazed."

"Good genes," Gomez said. "I come from good genes."

"Perhaps," Fish agreed. "Now the authorities, both the Metro Police and the FBI, are anxious to question you. I can honestly see no reason why they should not. What do you have to say about that?"

"I want to talk to them. I *do*. The sooner the better. I got a lot to tell them."

"Very well. I'll let them know."

Within the hour, both Vitelli and Maddox were interviewing Gomez.

"Okay, Alvaro," Vitelli began, pulling out a recording device. Maddox grinned, pulled out his smartphone to record the conversation as well.

"I'll be recording this," Vitelli continued. He spoke the time, day, and date into the microphone. "Tell us how you came to be holding Bobby Doyle prisoner."

And Gomez related his entire tale to them: his sister's pregnancy and stillbirth; their lawsuit; her suicide; his father's death; and his plan to wreak vengeance on Bobby Doyle. He held nothing back.

"I know what I did was wrong," he concluded. "I see that now. And I'm willing to pay for it. I did, after all, have every intention of killing Bobby, but I swear on my sister's grave, that I wasn't the one who killed him. What's today?" he asked. "What day is it?"

"Wednesday," Vitelli answered.

"Okay, then," Gomez said, "it was exactly a week ago that Bobby was killed. Shot with my gun. But it wasn't me who pulled the trigger. The night before, I had Bobby locked up and secure, right as rain, when Victor Korborov and his men raided my place and took both Bobby and me prisoner. They hauled us off to their hideout, and . . ."

Gomez then went on to relate the events of that Thursday night and the following morning.

"It was Wednesday morning. I was still tied up naked and bloody from the beating that bastard Vasyli had given me, when Korborov storms into the room where Bobby and me was, and shoots poor Bobby right in the head. Kills him. Right in front of me and his man Vasyli. Then Korborov, tells Vasyli some shit in Russian, and I watch as that animal Vasyli cuts Bobby Doyle's head off. I pissed myself, I can tell you, and I ain't ashamed to admit it."

"To be clear, you saw Viktor Korborov shoot and kill Bobby Doyle," Maddox reiterated.

"I did. And so did his goon, Vasyli."

"And what happened next?"

"Not a lot for the rest of the day. Just me, tied to that chair, and Bobby's headless body, his arms still shacked to that support column. Sometime later—I know it was nighttime, 'cause it was dark when we got outside—Vasyli came with some other guys and they untied me, tied my hands behind my back, and then unshackled what was left of Bobby's corpse. Then they hauled us down to a van, threw us into the back, and Vasyli drove us off to someplace in the city.

"First Vasyli drags Bobby's body out and dumps it," Gomez continued, "then he hauls me out. I was stiff as hell, and it was wicked cold. He duckwalks me over to where Bobby was, ties a plastic bag over my head, shoves me down next to Bobby, and steps on my back, pinning me to the ground. With the bag over my head, I'm struggling, trying to get air, and feel something sharp and hard in my mouth. Vasyli had shoved me face down on some rocks. I bit down on the one in my mouth and chewed open a hole so's I could breathe. I could get *some* air, but not much. I'm not sure what happened after that. I guess I must have passed out or whatever. That's all I remember until I woke up here in the hospital."

"That's plenty," Vitelli said, and Maddox nodded in agreement. "We'll get your statement written up in the form of a deposition, and you can sign it. You will sign it, right?"

"I will," Gomez said.

"WE'VE GOT HIM!" MADDOX was jubilant. "We've got that bastard, Korborov."

"Do we?" Vitelli said. "What we have is the testimony of an admitted kidnapper, a man who admitted he had every intention of killing Bobby Doyle himself. A decent defense attorney would tear his testimony to pieces."

"So how does Gomez then end up in an empty lot, almost dead, with a plastic bag around his head?"

183

"Could have staged it maybe? I don't know. But, according to Gomez, Korborov's man, Vasyli, saw the whole thing too. Maybe we can turn him," Vitelli said.

"Don't know about that. Korborov's men are fiercely loyal. But maybe. Meanwhile, we'd better concentrate on keeping Alvaro Gomez alive."

"Yes," Vitelli agreed. "We had better!"

Chapter 62

Around 7:00 PM Wednesday evening, four men entered Metro General Hospital. Each was a little overdressed for the cooler weather, in that each wore a full-length gray wool overcoat. Each man carried what appeared to be a large box of chocolates in one hand, and a bouquet of flowers in the other. One of the four men was very large, and stood a full head above the others, none of whom was exactly small.

They were greeted at the entry kiosk by one of the volunteers who worked at the hospital, a silver-haired woman with a broad smile. "Can I help you gentlemen?" she asked.

"No thank you," the large man said. "We know where we are going. Seeing an old friend."

"How lovely," she said, still smiling as they passed by. She couldn't help but notice the big man had spoken with a foreign accent. *Slavic,* she thought.

The four headed straight up to the west side elevators and got on the next one headed up, riding it to the fourth floor. When they left the elevator, they noted that the entire floor appeared empty: the nurse's station was deserted, and the nearby rooms were bare. There were no beds, no tables, no monitors, no equipment. Above all, there wasn't a single person in sight—which was just as they expected.

Besides the lighting over the nursing station, only one of the corridors radiating from the station was lit. They headed to that corridor.

Peering down that hallway, they could see four armed men at the far end of the corridor, sitting on gray plastic chairs outside one of the rooms. The entire length of the corridor was otherwise bare. While they didn't seem very alert, the other four did look up, and stand up, as soon as the four men in overcoats entered the corridor.

"*Uspokoysya*, stay calm," the big man said to the others. They began to walk, four abreast, slowly toward the other four men at the end of the hallway. Those four men were guards in full body armor, brandishing M4 rifles. Three of them stood up quickly, and assumed positions athwart the hallway, their rifles held close to their chests. The fourth was on a walkie-talkie, alerting the standby SWAT team.

When the two groups were about twenty feet apart, one of the three guards brought his rifle up to the ready, and said, "Hold it right there. Stop! Arms above your heads, gentlemen, and keep your hands where I can see them."

Vasyli and the others stopped and raised their chocolate boxes and floral bouquets above their heads as ordered. "Cover me," the fourth guard said as he set his walkie-talkie down and moved forward to examine the intruders. To his credit, he went straight to the tallest and largest man, Vasyli, and said, "Okay, sir, slowly now, please put your box and your flowers down on the floor."

Vasyli did as he was ordered, stooping down to do so, the hint of a smile on his round face. He stood up and slowly began to unbutton his overcoat. "What are you doing? the guard, agitated, asked, "I didn't tell you to open your coat!"

Vasyli spoke, still slowly unbuttoning his coat, "I am just showing you that I am unarmed," he said. He opened his coat, holding its lapels out wide in his outstretched hands. "You may frisk me if it makes you feel more comfortable," Vasyli said, "even if it *is* a probable violation of my civil rights."

"Your civil rights be damned," the guard said, dropping all veneer of civility, and frisked Vasyli, who stood submitting calmly. "He's clean," he announced to his compatriots, who were still standing well behind him, with their rifles now all at the ready. "I'll do the others," he said, and proceeded to the next man.

Just then there was a commotion as a Metro Police SWAT team, a squad of six men in full body armor, M4s at the ready, noisily entered the hallway, stopping about twenty feet from the Russians, and cutting off any possible escape route. "Easy now, gentlemen," the one guard said to Vasyli and the others, whose sudden apprehension and nervous agitation was obvious. "Our back-up won't bother you unless you do something stupid," and he continued frisking the four Russians.

It wasn't until the guard frisked the fourth man that he found a pistol at the small of the man's back, jammed into his belt. "He's got a gun!" he shouted, and his three comrades and the SWAT team raised their rifles, now aimed and ready to open fire.

"Easy," Vasyli begged. "Easy, please." Then, to the offender in Russian, "Pieter, you fool, why do you have a gun? I told you, 'No weapons!' "

"I'm sorry, Vasyli," the man replied. "If any shooting started, I just didn't wish to be defenseless." Pieter, his arms still raised, at least had the presence of mind to stand still while the examiner extracted the pistol from his belt.

"Pieter, you are an idiot," Vasyli said. "You almost got us killed."

The guards and the SWAT team members heard what Vasyli said, but those who listened carefully only recognized the word "idiot," which is the same in both English and Russian.

"*Mne zhal.* I'm sorry," Pieter responded.

"Okay," the guard said, "now they're all clean." The three others behind him, along with the SWAT squad, all of whom had been pointing their rifles, now slowly lowered them. "Okay," he continued, still addressing the Russians, "you can lower your arms now, but keep your hands out in front of you where I can see them."

Vasyli and the others complied.

That was a close call, Vasyli mused. *Viktor, your plan for this little diversion almost got all of us killed, thanks to Pieter. I still think we should have confronted these smug bastards with Kalashnikovs blazing! Let us hope the second part of your scheme goes according to plan.*

Chapter 63

At the same time, and in another part of the hospital, Alexzander Popov was about to prove his value to the Russian organization. He had been given an assignment by Viktor Korborov himself, and was about to prove that he was capable of doing far more than just observing and reporting.

In the breast pocket of Popov's scrubs was a full syringe of fentanyl, enough to kill a horse. His mission was to deliver the drug into the veins of the patient sleeping peacefully in room 282.

Day and night, the east wing of the second floor of Metro General was a busy place. It was there that stroke and brain trauma patients were housed. If you were going to undergo brain surgery, you were assigned a room on the second floor, east wing.

It was Popov's regular shift, and he didn't get off until midnight, but Viktor had stressed that he needed to get to Alvaro Gomez as close to 7:20 as possible. The irony of his being assigned to take out the man who he had fingered in the first place, was not lost on Popov. *This is somehow fitting,* he thought. *I first find him, and then I kill him!*

His presence in the wing would probably go entirely unnoticed. Orderlies came and went, night and day, every day, in all parts of the hospital. Wheeling patients in and out, moving beds and equipment about, setting up and breaking down. And Alexzander had always made it a habit to keep as much to himself as possible. He didn't fraternize, not even with his fellow orderlies, and, outside of his immediate supervisor and a few others, only a few people in the hospital recognized him, let alone knew his name. Popov didn't even have a regular girlfriend; he had always been a loner, and he preferred it that way. He paid for sex whenever he couldn't deny his needs.

The nurse's station he had passed was manned, and, as usual, the hallway was brightly lighted. There were the usual comings and goings. Nurses and nurse's aides passed by him, nodding and smiling, but not really seeing him, not recognizing him. The door to room 282 was ajar; Popov slipped unnoticed into the darkened room, shutting the door behind him, and moved silently toward the figure lying in the bed.

Chapter 64

"All right, who are you people?" the SWAT team leader asked.

"We are just visitors, four men visiting family, Pieter's mother, Mrs. Obolensky, in room 481. See? We were bringing chocolates and flowers!"

"Room 481 is at the other end of this floor, in the east wing, Commander," one of the four floor guards explained.

"Call down and find out who's in room 481, will you?" he asked.

"Sure," the guard said. "Back in a minute."

It took more than a minute, but the guard returned and said, "There's a Katya Obolensky in room 481, Commander."

"Right," the SWAT team leader said, "but that doesn't explain why her son, Pieter, here, was carrying, now does it?"

"No, it doesn't, but concealed carry is legal in this state, Commander," the guard replied.

"If he has a permit for the firearm, it is. But look at this pistol. The serial number has been filed off. I seriously doubt our Mr. Obolensky has a permit for it."

You are truly an idiot, Pieter, Vasyli thought, but instead said "I'm sure this is all just a misunderstanding, officers. Pieter, here, is new to this country, and doesn't understand its rules."

"No excuse," the SWAT team leader replied, and then said to Pieter, "Mr. Obolensky, you are under arrest for possession of an illegal handgun," and he proceeded to recite his Miranda rights to Pieter.

As the SWAT team escorted Pieter off to the city jail, Vasyli and his other two companions were told they could go about their business, and that they would have to go back to the lobby and take the east wing elevators up to the fourth floor to visit Mrs. Obolensky. "We will do that," Vasyli said, and the three retrieved their chocolates and (now worse for wear) floral bouquets, and departed for the elevators back down to the lobby. *I wonder how Pieter will explain it when the police find out that his surname is not Obolensky?* Vasyli wondered.

Chapter 65

There was one thing Alexzander Popov needed to do before he stuck the needle into Alvaro Gomez. The monitoring device, to which Gomez was attached by a series of wires and sensors, had to be disconnected.

The machine sent a constant feed out to the nurse's station: Gomez's body temperature, pulse, respiration rate, blood oxygen level, and blood pressure. The moment the fentanyl in the syringe hit Gomez's heart, it would stop, and the monitor would flat line. Then the nurses would come running.

But Popov had set up and broken down these machines dozens of times, and he knew how to simply power the machine down without pulling the plug; then the monitor at the nurse's station would show only that the machine in room 282 was still connected to the patient, but had—for whatever reason—gone offline. This would not be an unusual occurrence, and there would be no cause for immediate panic. Nor would there be any need for Popov to beat a hasty retreat after killing Gomez. Popov powered the monitor down, and then turned his attention to his victim, lying peacefully, clearly visible even in the darkened hospital room.

Popov took the syringe from his breast pocket, removed the plastic cap that covered the needle, and plunged it into the neck of the person in the bed. His thumb pushed down on the plunger, and the poison flowed into his victim.

And then the room suddenly became brightly lighted. Popov saw that he had just injected a street-valued, thousand dollars' worth of fentanyl into a first-aid practice dummy.

"Hold it right there, you," Vitelli said, sitting in a visitor's chair, and pointing his pistol at an astonished Popov. Popov turned, as if to try and make it to the door, when he saw his way out was now blocked by a uniformed policeman.

"Hands where I can see them," Vitelli ordered, and, dropping the empty syringe on the floor, Popov raised his arms and clasped his hands together behind his neck, interlocking his fingers. He had been arrested before, in Russia, and he knew the drill.

Down the hall, in room 267, Alvaro Gomez slept peacefully while the uniformed policeman on watch inside that room fought to stay awake.

THAT VERY NIGHT, AS Popov was transported to a secure jail cell, arrest warrants were issued and served upon Viktor Korborov and his sidekick, Vasyli.

Chapter 66

Thursday morning dawned cloudy and drizzly, the air wet and cold. Vitelli went for a run anyway, and, when it was over, returned to his place with steam rising from his workout clothing. The two cats, Tristan and Isolde, fed and watered earlier, each greeted his return with a toothy yawn and resumed to their momentarily interrupted watch for wildlife outside the living room window. A shower, and then off to the office. This was to be a big day, with both Korborov and Vasyli being arraigned for, among other things, murder one: Korborov for Bobby Doyle, and Vasyli for Arnold Schuster and Horace Blake.

Alexzander Popov was not arraigned that morning; he could be held without arraignment for another day and a half. No official mention to the media had been made concerning the previous evening's attempt on the life of Alvaro Gomez. Nor was it publicized that he had been quietly transferred from his hospital bed, to an FBI safe house that very morning. Since his resident spy at the hospital, Popov, was in jail, the move had taken place without Korborov's knowledge. Vitelli hoped, that as far as *anyone* knew, Gomez was still under guard at Metro General.

The arraignments of Korborov and Vasyli went smoothly enough. Vasyli was held over without bail for the double murder; his DNA found on both corpses was considered by the judge to be compelling physical evidence. He was also held over for the assault and attempted murder of Alvaro Gomez. Again, his DNA on the surgical wipes used to cleanse the victim at the hospital was physical evidence.

Vitelli was less pleased with the judge's decision to release Viktor Korborov on a million dollars' bail. In that case, the judge had reasoned, there was only the recorded eyewitness testimony of Alvaro Gomez, an admitted kidnapper.

Of course, Korborov's bail was quickly made, and Korborov just as quickly left police custody. Before he left, however, he got word to Vasyli that he would have a first-rate lawyer assigned to his case before the day was over. Vasyli trusted Korborov, and was positive that, somehow, his boss would get him released.

He would soon learn that his trust had been misplaced.

Chapter 67

Earlier, at four in the afternoon that same Thursday, Vitelli sat at the long table in the same conference room at Justyn Martyr Academy, where he and Maddox had interviewed Father William Dale the previous week. He had asked Sister Marie Therese, the school's principal, to arrange a meeting between Sister Lucy Simic and himself. She had said she would, but chided him, saying, "You know Sister Lucy is not in a prison. If you wish to speak to her in the future, you have only to call the school and ask her yourself!"

"Yes, Sister," Vitelli had replied, but prevailed on Sister Marie Therese to set up the meeting anyway, which she did. And the meeting was that very afternoon, after classes were over for the day.

She entered the room dressed identically as she had been when he saw her in the hallway that Tuesday morning, nine days earlier: in a clean, crisp white habit. Her brunette hair was covered by the cowl and the veil, but there was no mistaking that pretty face, those big brown eyes. There was no other possibility now. Vitelli was absolutely positive that Sister Lucy and Leona Barrett, "The Dry Cleaner," were one and the same.

"Hello, Richie," she said, as she entered the room. "I wasn't sure you had seen me the other day, when I saw you in the hallway after Mass let out. Have you come here to arrest me?" She calmly took a seat at the table opposite him, and, once seated, folded her hands on the table.

"You *saw* me?" Vitelli said, "And you're still here?"

"Where am I going to go? I'm here. It's where I *should* be."

"Lee, you're wanted for multiple murders. You're facing life in prison at the very least. You were safely out of the country, and nobody knew where you were. You were home free. Of all the places in the world, what in blazes are you doing back here, back in this country, back in *this* city?"

She smiled the very same smile that had captivated him some two years earlier. "Yeah. Ironic, isn't it? My order operates a dozen or so schools around the country, and another dozen or so in Europe, and they send me here. I had no choice, of course, you go where they send you. You go where you're needed."

"Com'on, Lee, you could have run anytime. You could have at least refused to come here."

"I couldn't really. I'd taken a vow of obedience. A temporary vow, maybe, but a vow nonetheless. I've learned to take such vows seriously. When they sent me here, I prayed you wouldn't find me—what are the chances, after all? But God has a sense of humor." She smiled. "Or justice, maybe. So here you are."

"Yeah. Here I am." He gazed at her in silence for a bit. "Okay, tell me how all this happened. How did you end up as a religious sister?"

"Well," she reminisced, "I was living the so-called good life in the Caribbean, and was totally going out of my mind after just a couple of months. You can only drink so many Mai-tais and bed so many beach boys before that gets really old. Then I got a visit from a Franciscan priest, Father Stephen Obutu. Father Stephen is from Africa—Kenya—he can be very persuasive. He was starting a school for the Island kids, and was begging for money. I had more than I could possibly spend, so I gave him some."

She smiled again, the memory apparently pleasant. "As the school was being built, and Father was setting up classes wherever he could find room, he invited me to come see what my contribution had accomplished. Of course, I knew it was just so he could ask for more money, but I went anyway. There were only three nuns there as teachers—sisters from my order—and they had their hands full. But the kids were so lovely, and so eager to learn! So, I gave Father more money, and started teaching them myself. I fell in love with those kids, and teaching them was pure joy. I loved watching the lights come on behind those beautiful, bright eyes every time they learned something new."

Another smile. "And I found out I'm a *very* good teacher, and I *do* have an excellent background in science, after all! Well, I got hooked. By the end of the first year, I had gone through instruction to become Catholic, and applied for admission into the order. They must have been desperate, because I was accepted." She paused.

"I found out later that they checked out my background completely, but there were no active warrants out for Lucy Simic, and I used my birth name on the application. The order accepted the fact that my adoptive parents' name, Barnett, the surname on my college degree, was just as authentic, and they never questioned it. So, here I am, *Sister* Lucy Simic."

"And all the money?"

"Gave it away. All of it. To people and things that needed it. A vow of poverty goes along with that vow of obedience, you know."

"So I've heard," Vitelli said. "Chastity, too." Sister Lucy smiled. Vitelli stewed for a minute, deep in thought. "Shit, Lee," he eventually said, "what am I going to do with you?"

"Whatever you must," she replied. "I'm not going anywhere. You have your duty to do, and I understand that. Do whatever you must, Richie." She looked genuinely concerned, not for herself, but for him, and his apparent dilemma.

They sat together for a while. Then Vitelli got up from the table. "Well, Sister," he said, "I've got to go now. I guess I'll see you around."

"Please do," she said. "I'll be right here."

Chapter 68

Alexzander Popov was arraigned first thing on Friday morning. His prints and mug shot had been routinely sent out to Interpol and law enforcement agencies nationwide, and a hit had already come back from New York. It seems that Alexzander Popov was just one of several aliases used by one Alexei Pavlenko, a native of Chechnya. Pavlenko was the subject of an outstanding warrant issued by the State of New York for jumping bail on an aggravated assault charge.

At the arraignment, Pavlenko stood accused of attempted murder; his lawyer, one Arthur Kronsnoble, had him plead not guilty to all charges.

Confronted with the outstanding warrant, and given the testimony of two police officers who had witnessed him administering over a thousand milliliters of fentanyl to a first-aid dummy he thought was Alvaro Gomez, the judge ordered Pavlenko to be held without bail, awaiting trial. His lawyer tried to make a case for bail, citing the fact that Pavlenko had never been previously accused of a crime in this state, and the judge practically laughed him out of court.

Friday morning also found Korborov's henchman Vasyli alone in a high-security federal jail cell. Vasyli was a touch claustrophobic, and hated jail cells of any kind. Still, this cell, unlike several he had occupied in Russia and elsewhere, was at least clean and dry; it was even air-conditioned.

Around ten, his outer, solid, cell door was opened and a guard announced, "Your lawyer is here. Hands through the slot." Vasyli stared incomprehensibly. The guard pointed to the horizontal opening in the second, barred door. "Both hands. Stick them through here." Vasyli complied, and was cuffed.

Only then was the inner door unlocked and Vasyli allowed to enter the corridor. He followed the guard to a small consultation room off the same corridor. There was a large wire-reenforced glass window between the room and the hallway; the room's occupants could be seen, but their conversation remained private. Inside the room, seated at a small table, was a small, thin, balding, bespectacled man in the three-piece, blue, pin-striped suit. He rose to greet Vasyli as he was ushered inside.

"Vasyli?" the man asked, and when Vasyli nodded, he said, "I'm Arthur Kronsnoble. Mister Korborov has arranged for me to be your lawyer."

Vasyli grunted his approval and sat across from his lawyer, as the guard closed the door behind them. Another enclosed space. The large window to the hallway should have helped, but it did not, because the guard was standing there, watching. "When are you going to get me out of this place?" Vasyli asked.

"No time soon," Kronsnoble answered truthfully. "I'll be honest with you, Vasyli, the state has a pretty much, ironclad case against you. Your blood was found on four men: one, Horace Blake, was beaten to death; another, Arnold Schuster, first beaten, then smothered to death with a plastic bag; the third man beaten, and *almost* smothered to death. *And* the third man, Alvaro Gomez, has identified you as the man who beat him and attempted to murder him. And, finally, the fourth man, Bobby Doyle, was first kidnapped and then found decapitated next to Gomez. The kidnapping makes at least that part of this a federal case, and that's why you're in here and not in state custody. You'll have to admit none of that sounds very good for you."

"My own fault for not finishing the job on Gomez," Vasyli said.

Kronsnoble winced, and said, "I'll pretend I didn't hear that."

"So, my first-rate, defense lawyer, how are you going to get me off?"

"I just finished explaining to you, didn't I, Vasyli? The case against you is too strong. God himself couldn't get you off."

"So Viktor *pays* somebody, and gets me off, no?"

"No. That may be the way things work in Russia, Vasyli, but not here—certainly not in a Federal prison, and especially not in such a high-profile case as this. The entire country is appalled by what happened to Bobby Doyle. The media are screaming for blood. And right now you're being made for all three of these murders, including Bobby Doyle. You can add aggravated assault and attempted murder to that."

"I did not kill Bobby Doyle. Viktor did that. The other things, maybe, but not that one. That one is on Viktor."

"Okay," Kronsnoble said. "Here's the thing, Vasyli. Two murders or three, not much difference—especially if you plead guilty to all three, and throw yourself on the mercy of the court. That way, you might just avoid the death penalty—capital punishment is still legal in this state."

"So, I say I am guilty for everything," Vasyli said in his accented English, "Viktor gets off, and I maybe not be executed, but put into jail for how long?"

"Thirty to life," his lawyer said matter-of-factly.

"How is that?"

"Thirty years to life. That means the judge sentences you to life in prison, but you'll be up for parole after serving thirty years."

Vasyli sat stunned. *Thirty years!* he thought. *If I live through it, they may let me out after thirty years! I will be a doddering old man! And that's only if I live that long, and if they even let me out after thirty years!*

Kronsnoble observed his client. Korborov had led him to believe that Vasyli would be more compliant than this. Finally, he said, "Look, Vasyli, think about it. As it sits right now, at the arraignment, as in any murder case, a not guilty plea was automatically entered for you. That plea stands unless you reverse it. You're being held without bail until your trial. That could take months. Plenty of time to make up your mind. I'll be back in touch. Meanwhile, don't talk to anybody—not to the police, and certainly not to the FBI—unless I'm there to represent you. Got that?"

When Vasyli nodded that he understood, the lawyer rose, and signaled to the guard that the session was over.

Stunned, Vasyli remained seated until Kronsnoble had left, and the guard came in to take him back to his cell.

Chapter 69

While Vasyli was being introduced to reality, Vitelli sat at his desk and wondered whether he had done the right thing. *It's still not too late to go back there and arrest her.* But, actually, he knew it was. If he was going to arrest Leona Barrett, he needed to have done it yesterday, the day he had confronted her, and had definitely identified her as the woman they called "The Dry Cleaner." *Yeah, if I was going to do it, I should have done it then and there. Really is too late now. I may have just made the biggest mistake of my life.*

And so now she's back here. But why? Why, when she was home free and unable to be touched by anyone? Unless of course, the conversion she described is authentic. It must be. She's taken vows to become a nun, and it was her order that sent her here — she had no choice. She had to either quit or obey. She could have quit, but she said didn't. Why else would she come back here?

Well, she better have changed, or I'm in deep shit — really deep shit!

FOR LUNCH THAT DAY, Vitelli visited the Sabrett hot dog stand that had operated right outside the Metro Police HQ for as long as Vitelli could remember. The stand was owned by an Hispanic guy with a bushy black moustache, and a mop of wavy black hair. The two men, Vitelli and the hot dog vendor, had developed an informal, friendly relationship, even if neither actually knew the other by name.

"The usual, *Hermano*," Vitelli said. "One with everything. I missed you — last week, was it? I was salivating for one of your hot dogs, but you weren't here. That never happens!"

"Sorry, Lieutenant," the vendor said, as he served up one of his foot-long, all-beef, kosher-style dogs with a generous helping of fresh sauerkraut, and a special tomato-based onion sauce. "My little girl had her *quinceanera*, her fifteenth-birthday celebration, that weekend, and her mother and I promised her we'd take her to the zoo the following Monday. She loves the zoo. I couldn't get my brother to fill in for me, like he usually does, so I wasn't here. Only missed that one Monday. Sorry."

"No big deal. *Quinceaneras* are special, and a promise is a promise. Give me an ice tea, will you?"

"Sure thing. Here you go. That'll be eight-fifty."

"Here's ten, keep it."

"Thanks, Lieutenant."

That has to be the ten-thousandth time for that very same transaction, Vitelli mused, *but it's certainly been worth it. Best damn hot dog in the city!*

Back at his desk, next to the widow that was so dingy it barely let in any light, even on the brightest days, Vitelli again began mulling over yesterday's visit to the Justin Martyr Academy. The ringing telephone broke his train of thought. "Vitelli," he said, answering it.

"It's Eric, Rich," Maddox said. "Tell me, you think we can get this guy Vasyli to turn, get him to give up Korborov?"

"I don't know. But my guess would be that Korborov has lawyered him up, long since. No way Vasyli will talk to us without his lawyer present, and no mob lawyer is going to let his client finger the man who's paying him. We can certainly try, but my guess is that the whole thing would be an exercise in futility."

"Yeah, well, you're probably right. But I think we'll have to make the effort anyway. The only reason Korborov is out on bail is that the case against him is based solely on Gomez's testimony—the guy who kidnapped Bobby Doyle in the first place. If we can get Vasyli to cave on his boss, corroborate Gomez's testimony that it was Korborov that shot and killed Bobby Doyle, then we can put Korborov away for good."

"True, but that's a big 'if.'"

"Rich, we *have* to try."

"Okay, set it up."

WHILE VITELLI AND MADDOX were on the telephone, so also were Viktor Korborov and Arthur Kronsnoble.

"You are on a burner phone, right?" Korborov was saying.

"What do you take me for, Viktor?! I am not an amateur."

"Very well then, counselor. You spoke to Vasyli?"

"I did." An awkward silence followed.

"And?" Korborov asked, breaking the silence.

"And I don't think he's going to go along with it— pleading guilty, that is."

"What do you mean he is not going to go along with it? Vasyli is a soldier. He has to. This is what a soldier does."

"Maybe not this time."

Korborov blew up, shouting into the phone, "Well you just better make sure he does, do you understand? This is Vasyli we are talking about! And Vasyli does exactly what he is told!

"Yes, Viktor," Kronsnoble answered. *But maybe not this time.*

Chapter 70

"Anubis, it is Viktor."

"Yes, Viktor, to what do I owe the pleasure?"

"I need your help. To do something only you are capable of doing, no?"

"What is that?"'

"The *politsiya* have made me for the Bobby Doyle killing. Right now, they have only the Gomez boy as a witness. I am out on bail only because Gomez kidnapped Doyle in the first place, and the judge said he was not a reliable witness. But my man Vasyli was also there, and he is *also* a witness."

"How inconvenient for you, Viktor. But you killed my team's star quarterback, Viktor, and you have cost me a great deal of money. Why ever should I help you?"

"Because I can pay you to."

"Excellent reasoning, my friend, excellent reasoning. Provided, of course, that you can pay me *enough*. Now what is it that you want?"

"I want both the Gomez boy and Vasyli dead."

"What? I can understand your wanting Gomez dead, but why Vasyli? He's *your* man, after all."

"It was Vasyli who did not finish the job I gave him, to kill Gomez, in the first place. I would not be in this situation if he did as he was told. Now he might well turn on me and make some arrangement with the *politsiya* for better treatment. That is why."

"Ah, now I understand. But I'm afraid I can't help you with silencing either of them, Viktor. I know for a fact that Vasyli is being held in solitary confinement in a maximum-security cell in the federal prison. And Gomez is in an FBI safe house somewhere in the city, and not even my contacts in the Metro Police Department know *his* whereabouts. I'm sorry, Viktor, no amount of money can buy you the impossible. But perhaps I can help you in another way."

"I'm listening."

"I can get you out of the country—this very day. Take you to a place where not even the FBI can touch you."

"Where, and how much?"

"Cuba. It will take a million to have the Cuban authorities look the other way and let you into the country unhindered—especially if you transfer your considerable fortune into a Cuban bank once you arrive in Havana. Then there will be another quarter million for my trouble. Making such arrangements on short notice is expensive. It includes my fee, of course, and a quarter million is a mere pittance."

"So. You can get me to Cuba for one a quarter million, and I can leave right away?"

"I can."

"I will wire you the money within the hour. Make it happen."

"Very well. There's a private airport just south of the city in Madisonville. Martin Airfield. I will have a plane fueled up and waiting for you in under two hours. From there, you'll be flown to another private airfield just outside of Port Everglades, Florida. A fast boat will be waiting for you to make the two-hundred-or-so-mile trip from Port Everglades to Havana. By this time tomorrow, you'll be ensconced at the Gran Hotel Manzana Kempinski La Habana. Sound good?"

"*Very* good. I'll wire you the money and set out for this Martin Airfield. And thank you, Anubis."

"My pleasure, Viktor. Enjoy Havana."

THAT VERY EVENING A small private plane, with a pilot and a single passenger onboard, took off from a private airport in Madisonville en route to another private airport just outside of Port Everglades, Florida. Its sole passenger was Viktor Korborov.

Chapter 71

It was a Saturday morning, and Vitelli had just gone for a run. It was damp and cold out, and the run had been invigorating. He had showered and was thinking of going out to breakfast when the phone rang. It was Eric Maddox.

"Just got a call from the prison where we are holding Vasyli. He wants to talk."

"When?"

"This morning. Ten o'clock."

"Okay. Will his lawyer be there?"

"He says he's waiving his rights and doesn't want him there."

"Sounds serious. Now I'll be there for sure."

Vitelli stopped off at the City Bagel Shoppe and got a toasted plain bagel with cream cheese and smoked salmon to eat on the way.

AT THE FEDERAL PRISON, Vitelli and Eric Maddox were waiting in the same small interview room used by Vasyli and his lawyer the previous day. A manacled Vasyli was brought into the room under guard. Only after Vasyli was seated and his manacles affixed to a stout steel ring on the interview table, did the guard leave. Then, he stood outside the room and observed the three men inside through the large reinforced-glass window.

"Well, Vasyli, you said you wanted to see us, so we're here," Maddox began, stating the obvious. "But before you begin," he continued, as he placed his phone on the table, "I want you to know I will be recording our conversation. Do you consent to this?"

Vasyli nodded his head in affirmation.

"You have to say it, Vasyli," Maddox said.

"Yes," Vasyli said aloud.

Maddox went on to name the people in the room and state the date and time. "You must understand that you have the right to have your lawyer present. I understand that you have waived this right. Do you waive your right to have a lawyer present, Vasyli?"

"Yes."

"Good. Now tell us why you wanted to speak to us this morning."

"I want to make a deal."

"What kind of a deal?"

"You know what kind. I tell you what I know, and you people let me go."

"That's not going to happen, Vasyli. We can prove that you are responsible for two murders for sure—Schuster and Blake, and possibly even a third, Bobby Doyle. And it's for sure that you attempted to murder Alvaro Gomez. That's at least two counts of murder one, and one definite assault with intent to murder. In this state, Vasyli, you're facing the death penalty. And, besides, there's a kidnapping involved, and that makes it federal. No way we can let you go free. Even if you plead, you'll at least do some time, no matter what," Maddox said.

"I know all that. That much my shitty lawyer already told me. But, if I cannot get off entirely, then what is it that you can do for me?"

"That depends. What kind of information do you have for us?"

"I can tell you who really killed Bobby Doyle."

"Well, Vasyli, we are pretty sure that *you* did," Maddox lied. "Your DNA was all over the body."

"I cut his head off, but he was already dead. Now tell me what you can do for me, if I tell you who really killed Bobby Doyle."

214

"We can probably do a deal with the District Attorney to take the death penalty off the table."

"That is it? That is all you can do?"

"Maybe get a reduced sentence for your cooperation, but, honestly, that's up to the DA, not us. All Detective Vitelli and I can do is plead your case with him. But there's no getting around it, Vasyli. Two counts of murder one. You are at least going to do some time. Now, what exactly is it that you can do for us?"

"I can give up Viktor Korborov to you. I saw him shoot Bobby Doyle — put bullet in his brain. Viktor killed him, and I saw it. Then he told me to cut off Bobby Doyle's head."

"What about the other murders? Who told you to kill Arnold Schuster and Horace Blake?"

"Viktor did."

"And the attempted murder of Alvaro Gomez?"

"Again, Viktor."

"And you do everything Viktor Korborov tells you to?" Vitelli broke in testily.

"I do!" Vasyli snapped. "I am a soldier!"

"WELL," VITELLI SAID TO Maddox afterward, "We now at least have a pretty air-tight case against Korborov for Bobby Doyle's murder. Two eye witnesses. Pretty sure the DA will cut Vasyli some slack for that."

"Most likely," Maddox replied. "Let's go get Korborov."

"As soon as I can get another arrest warrant."

But even as quickly as Vitelli could get a judge to sign off on the warrant, and get a crew out to arrest Korborov, it was still too late. The cage door had been propped open, and that bird was long gone.

Chapter 72

Like all intelligent criminals, Viktor Korborov always had a "go bag" ready, should an immediate evacuation ever be required. He retrieved it from the bottom of his closet, along with the leather jacket that had twenty-five thousand dollars sewn into the lining. It took him no time at all to leave his mob headquarters behind and make his way south to Madisonville and Martin Airfield. The GPS unit in his Range Rover guided him directly to the place. He was there, waiting for the air crew that would fly him to Port Everglades within ninety minutes of having ended his telephone conversation with Anubis Cline.

His air "crew" turned out to be a single pilot, and the plane a single-engine, two-seater, an ancient Cessna 140. "She's old, but she's reliable," the pilot said to Korborov, after the two were seated and the plane was ready to take off. Korborov was not reassured, but felt he had no other alternative other than to stay the course Cline had mapped out for him.

"The trip is just under twelve hundred miles," the pilot said." If we could just fly straight though, we could be there in ten hours. But we gotta stop every four hours or so and fuel up, so there are two scheduled stops on the way. But you never mind that. Relax and get some sleep. We'll be in Florida in the morning, safe and sound, you'll see."

Korborov had never flown in a plane this small before, and while the pilot seemed to enjoy the bouncing and the gut-wrenching drops when it suddenly lost altitude, the whole experience only made him sick. He was thankful for being on solid ground at the first fuel stop, which was in God-only-knows-where, only to realize that he had to endure one more such hop before he could settle down, at least for a while, on permanently unmoving ground. He was far too ill to admire the brilliant sunrise from eight thousand feet just before the plane set down in Port Everglades.

Korborov was just getting his bearings when he and his "go bag" were picked up by a driver in a nondescript Ford Escort and driven to the port itself. The driver stopped the car next to a crude dock that seemed to have been hidden in a grove of palm trees somewhere on the coast. At the dock was tied a low, sleek, cigarette boat, powered by four powerful Mercury Marine outboard motors mounted on the transom. Korborov was met by a captain and a crew of two.

"Get in, sir," the captain said, speaking with a heavy Latin accent. "We have two hundred-forty miles to go from here to *La Habana*. So, get comfortable. The weather is perfect, and the sea is very calm. This boat can easily make forty knots, but is uncomfortable at that speed, so we will cruise at thirty. We should be in *La Habana* by dinnertime."

The boat cleared the dock and was in the Atlantic and headed south in no time. *So, this is what our idiot Captain thinks is a calm sea, is it? It seems to me there are many substantial hills and valleys in the water, and this boat bounces worse than that infernal plane!*

By noon, the boat was well clear of the Florida peninsula and out in the open water between the Florida Keys and Cuba. Despite the bouncing, Korborov had fallen into an exhausted sleep on a padded bench in the stern of the boat. He was startled awake only when the two crewmen lifted him off the bench and tossed him off the boat and into the Atlantic. He swallowed seawater as he went down, weighted by his leather jacket, only to kick to the surface seconds later, sputtering and coughing. He watched as his "go bag" was tossed in after him, and the boat took a sharp left turn and head back north.

"Buenas tardes, señor," the captain called after him, as he gunned the outboards, and the boat sped away.

Chapter 73

Sitting in front of the fireplace, beneath the gold urn that contained his ward's ashes, Anubis Cline carried on a conversation with her.

"But I do not understand, Abba, why even bother to dispose of Viktor Korborov? Certainly, the authorities had sufficient evidence to convict him of Bobby Doyle's murder. Why not just let him spend the next thirty years in jail?"

Because, my dear Jael, Korborov was impetuous, but he was not stupid. Sooner or later, he would have realized that it was me that goaded him into killing Doyle in the first place. Or he might have thought that I told the police that it was he who sent me Doyle's head.

"But you would never have told them that, at least not directly. That would only have implicated you in the murder as well. It was enough that you only pointed them in his direction by use of that Russian word."

Yes, there was that. And even that may have been going a bit too far. But I'm afraid I couldn't help myself. Sometimes I'm just a tad too clever for my own good! In any case, that is all academic now, in light of Korborov's impending sudden demise.

"I still do not see where that is more of an advantage then letting him rot in prison. After all, you do have some exposure in arranging for his death."

The advantage, Jael, is that a dead Korborov is in no way a threat to us. Remember that Viktor was a mob boss. Even in prison, with his teeth supposedly drawn, he could still bite. A word from him, an order conveyed, and a team of his Russian goons would be after us with mayhem in mind. As to my exposure in arranging his sudden demise, that is minimal. All arrangements were made at arm's length, and, with Korborov's one and a quarter *million dollars, I could afford to buy the very best. Professional people. Discreet and reliable. Good at what they do.*

Then Cline grunted. For him, that was laughing aloud.

The irony, Jael, is that Viktor paid me all that money to put him into his watery grave! No reason to give any of it to the Cubans, when he'll never set foot on the island! Isn't that just so precious?

"*Yes, Abba, as always, you are* extremely *clever!*"

Not clever enough, Cline thought, sighing. *I can only imagine the size of the fortune that Korborov had distributed between a bevy of banks in the Caribbean and South America. If I were all that clever, I would have figured out a way to get all that money as well.*

"*Must not beat yourself up, Abba.*"

No, Jael, I must learn not to be so greedy. I must teach myself to be content with what little I already have.

Chapter 74

Needless to say, that last Saturday evening, Vitelli was none too happy to learn that the arresting officers dispatched to pick up Viktor Korborov, came back to Metro Police Headquarters empty handed. But neither was he very surprised.

"Our bird has indeed flown the coop," Vitelli reported by telephone to Captain Parker at his home.

"What did you expect," was Parker's gruff answer, "when some do-gooder, numb-nuts judge lets a mobster on the loose on a million dollars' bail? We had Korborov dead to rights for Bobby Doyle's murder. Hell, a million bucks is nothing to a mob kingpin like Korborov. That idiot judge might just as well have bought him his plane ticket out of the country. Bet that rat bastard is in Venezuela, or someplace like that, by now."

"Most likely," Vitelli agreed. "His man, Vasyli, will be none too happy, though. With Korborov gone, his testimony against him will be far less valuable. And with Korborov in the wind, he might just figure he'll be more likely to suffer retaliation for turning state's evidence, and could just clam up. I know I probably would. Korborov, even on the lam, could have a *very* long reach."

"You may be right. What about that kid, Gomez? That little bastard is the one who set off this whole shitstorm! Think he might clam up too now?"

"I don't think so. I think Alvaro's gotten religion. But we'll see."

"Okay, Rich. Make the most of what's left of the weekend. Who do the Marauders play tomorrow? You know?"

"They don't. It's a bye week. They play New Orleans again next Thursday night on Prime. Should be a reasonably good game as long as McArdle stays healthy."

"Right. Well, see you on Monday, Rich."

"See you, Captain."

Chapter 75

Sunday morning started out with a cold driving rain, so Vitelli skipped the run. But he had gotten up early enough to feed the cats and then go running, so he took the extra time to cook himself a leisurely breakfast of sausage patties and over-medium eggs, eat it, and still make the ten o'clock Mass at St Anselm's.

It was, according to the parish bulletin, the Thirty-First Sunday in Ordinary Time—whatever that meant. The ceremony was fulfilling, as aways, and even the pastor's brief homily actually made sense for once. Vitelli had been to other Christian religious services, ones that centered around the minister's sermon, and had long ago decided that if Catholics went to Mass for the parish priest's sermon, the religion would have died out centuries ago. But, if asked, Vitelli would have been at loggerheads to explain why he was attracted to Mass. He only knew that the Mass was satisfying, and, for him at least, somehow complete.

Mass over, it was doughnut time in the narthex. This time he would resist the soft, yummy, sugar-glazed treats. He stood aside from the line hoping to see Pam there, but she was not in the line. Instead, there was a tap on his shoulder, and she was standing beside him, a vision in yellow and blue, her smile lighting up the place.

"Hi, Rich! How nice to see you again."

"Hello Pam." He was at a momentary loss as to what to say next, and felt stupid as soon as he said what he did say: "I looked for you last week, but you weren't here."

She either missed, or simply ignored, the banality.

"No, my brother and I drove up to Maryville last weekend to visit my mom and dad. Dad's health is not the greatest, so we go up there whenever we can."

"Ah, your parents. It's a long drive to Maryville. A couple of hours, isn't it?"

"Not the way John drives. My brother is a very conservative driver. Takes him at least an extra ten minutes to get us there."

"That's a good thing. Careful is good. I lost my folks just a few years ago, not long after Margie, my wife, died. That was not an easy time."

"No, I guess not. What happened? How did you lose them?"

"Road accident. Head-on collision with a semi. The truck driver had been on the road for twelve hours, and fell asleep at the wheel. Crossed the median."

"How tragic," she said. "I'm so sorry!"

Vitelli smiled a wan smile, said, "Well, enough of that," and changed the subject. "You guys doing brunch this morning? If you are, I'd like to join you."

"We are, and you are more than welcome to join us."

"Good. One thing before we go. This is—what—the third time we've met? And I still don't know your last name."

She broke into a full, throaty laugh. The other parishioners in the narthex turned to look at her; smiling, they shared in her mirth, despite not sharing the reason for it.

"Wagner," she said. "I go by my married name of Wagner."

Chapter 76

Monday morning, and Vitelli attended the disposition hearings for both Gomez and Vasyli.

The DA charged Vasyli with two counts of murder one: (Schuster and Blake); another on attempted murder (Gomez); another on assault and battery (Farnsworth); and on some minor charges (breaking and entering and stealing official documents). Vasyli was represented, again, by Arthur Kronsnoble, who plead for him: "Not guilty, on all counts."

As Vitelli had predicted, with Korborov on the loose, Vasyli had rejected the DA's offer of leniency in exchange for his eyewitness testimony against his old boss.

Gomez was represented by a public defender, an intense young man named Fletcher Ross, and was charged with the kidnapping and unlawful imprisonment of Bobby Doyle. In a plea deal, the DA had offered Gomez leniency in exchange for his testimony against Korborov and Vasyli, and he had accepted. *Not smart,* Vitelli thought. *He won't last long if they put him in with the general prison population.*

Ross entered the plea for Gomez: "Mr. Gomez pleads 'guilty as charged,' and the defendant throws himself on the mercy of the court."

The judge ordered Vasyli be held over for trial, and remanded Gomez be held over for sentencing.

"I COULD SMELL LUNCH from down the hall," Sister Lucy said, as she entered the academy conference room.

Vitelli just looked up at her and grinned. Lunch was to be a brief affair; Sister Lucy was between classes, and she had a General Chemistry class to teach at 1:10 that afternoon.

"You didn't!" she exclaimed. "You brought Sabrett hot dogs from the stand outside your office! How thoughtful!"

"I did," Vitelli acknowledged, "loaded with all the fixin's, and some iced tea to wash them down. I'd have brought you some beer instead, but I didn't think your new profession would allow it."

She smiled, and chided him gently, "I'm still *in* the world, Richie—just not *of* it!"

IT WASN'T THE GRAN Hotel Manzana Kempinski La Habana, but it would have to do. The place at least, located on a byway off Havana's Via Blanca, was private, reasonably clean, and cheap. It had enough space for Viktor Korborov to lay out the money he had stashed in the lining of his leather jacket so it could dry.

There were twenty-five packets of ten, one-hundred-dollar bills each, a pretty sight, even if, laid out as they were, the bills did take up every surface in the room. *How thoughtful of the American government to print their money on such high-quality paper!* thought Korborov. *One might have worried that they would turn into mush after soaking in the sea for a day and a half. But, no, good as new when the bills do finally dry out.*

Korborov had indeed drifted at sea for a day and a half before he was sighted and rescued by a Cuban fishing boat. His command of Spanish was poor, but he had been able to convey to the boat's captain that he was fleeing from the United States government and was seeking asylum in Cuba. It was another day and a half before the boat had set into Cojimar, and yet another before Korborov was able to make his way into downtown Havana, ostensibly (or so he told the boat captain) to contact the Cuban government authorities and officially apply for asylum.

You tried, Anubis Cline, you tried to kill me, and I was a fool to ever trust you in the first place. But you did, at least, manage to get me quickly out of the States. For that I owe you, but now —

now — *you owe me so much more. And you will pay, Anubis Cline, how you will pay!*

About the Author

Gene Masters is a retired consulting engineer living in East Tennessee with his wife, Ruth. They have two grown daughters, and two grandchildren. He is the author of several technical treatises, including his doctoral dissertation, and seven novels.

Masters received a commission in the U.S. Navy on graduation from Notre Dame, and his first tour of duty was aboard a transport in the Western Pacific. His second tour was aboard a recommissioned and updated diesel-electric submarine, the USS *Angler*. *Angler* was originally commissioned in 1943, and made seven war patrols in the Pacific before being decommissioned. Her updating to an SSK-class boat in the 1950s fitted her for operation against cold war submarine adversaries with advanced soundproofing and sonar. Masters left *Angler* and active duty after a Mediterranean tour. Later Naval Reserve assignments included the diesel-electric submarines USS *Manta* and the USS *Ling*.

After active duty, Masters pursued a career in engineering, and served in various companies until settling into a career as a consulting engineer. He retired in 2009. Readers can reach the author via email at 240boat@gmail.com, and view his website at *www.genemasters.net*.